"A suspenseful,   es
in childlike ter   as
well as the noti

                                                        ok

"Most interesting are the themes of guilt and evil that
motivate the story in terms that children can well
understand."

—School Library Journal

"The writing is vivid and swift as it reveals the strange
events in a special time for 11-year-old Jenny Ehrenteil . . . a thoroughly likeable, well-rounded story."
—Publishers Weekly

"Both Jenny's story and the diary narrative are vig-
orous and effective: the two are nicely knit. Recommended."

—Bulletin of the Center for Children's Books

DORIS ORGEL was born in Vienna, Austria. When Hitler
came to power her family managed to escape, first to
Yugoslavia, then to England, where she lived for a
time with a family not unlike the one described in
A Certain Magic. Mrs. Orgel is the author of Next
Door to Xanadu and The Mulberry Music. She lives
in Westport, Connecticut.

THE LAUREL-LEAF LIBRARY brings together under a single imprint outstanding works of fiction and
nonfiction particularly suitable for young adult readers, both in and out of the classroom. The series is
under the editorship of Charles F. Reasoner, Profes-
sor of Elementary Education, New York University.

ALSO AVAILABLE IN LAUREL-LEAF LIBRARY:

THE CRYSTAL NIGHTS *by Michele Murray*

ZIA *by Scott O'Dell*

TRANSPORT 7-41-R *by Dianne Glaser*

WHY HAVE THE BIRDS STOPPED SINGING?
by Zoa Sherburne

INTRODUCING SHIRLEY BRAVERMAN
by Hilma Wolitzer

THE SUMMER PEOPLE *by John Rowe Townsend*

GOOD NIGHT, PROF, DEAR *by John Rowe Townsend*

HEADS YOU WIN, TAILS I LOSE
by Isabelle Holland

LOVE AND DEATH AND OTHER JOURNEYS
by Isabelle Holland

A Certain Magic

DORIS ORGEL

LAUREL-LEAF LIBRARY

Published by
Dell Publishing Co., Inc.
1 Dag Hammarskjold Plaza
New York, New York 10017

Copyright © 1976 by Doris Orgel

All rights reserved. No part of this book may be reproduced in any form or by any means without the prior written permission of The Dial Press, 1 Dag Hammarskjold Plaza, New York, New York 10017, excepting brief quotes used in connection with reviews written specifically for inclusion in a magazine or newspaper.

Laurel-Leaf Library ® TM 766734, Dell Publishing Co., Inc.

ISBN: 0-440-91339-X

Reprinted by arrangement with The Dial Press.
Printed in the United States of America
First Laurel-Leaf printing—October 1978
Second Laurel-Leaf printing—February 1979

To my
Mother and Father

Jenny lay, *A Kids' Guide to London* propped on her knees, in her special hollow on Aunt Trudl's soft old couch with the twenty-three scatter cushions scattered around. Afternoon sunlight poured into the room. Apricot Jones nuzzled against Jenny's sweater and purred. I'd purr too, Jenny thought. She felt cozy as always up here, yet also excited, wishing the time would hurry up.

Then suddenly some awful thoughts came uninvited into her head: What if something spoiled it all? What if *I* did something to spoil everything? Like, leave a window wide open while I was up here alone taking care of the cats . . . and Murrna fell down . . . nine flights down! Or suppose I was in the bedroom-study . . . and there was a power failure, the lights went out . . . and I took some matches . . . and I lit some candles . . . and by accident a whole bunch of pages of some really hard translation Aunt Trudl might have been working on for months got burned to ashes. . . .

"Cuckoo, cuckoo, cuckoo, cuckoo," the cuckoo came out of the clock and called.

He was right, it was cuckoo thinking thoughts like that. Jenny looked at her wrist watch. Hey, he was right about the time, too! Aunt Trudl's friend Silverman had tried and tried to fix that old clock. What do you know, he'd finally done it!

The cuckoo hopped back in.

Jenny did some mental math, and figured out, Sixty-seven more hours till we're on the plane.

This was Tuesday of the week before spring vacation. In three more days, on Friday, while the other kids were still at school, she would be taking an eleven o'clock flight to London. She had been looking forward to that more than to anything in her whole life. One thing was wrong, though: Aunt Trudl wasn't coming.

Jenny got up from the couch and went toward Aunt Trudl's bedroom-study, calling to her, "You can still change your mind! Daddy checked with the airline, they said there's still room on the plane."

"That was nice of him," Aunt Trudl said.

Jenny went in there. Aunt Trudl was packing a suitcase.

She *did* change her mind, Jenny thought. Oh, good, I'm so glad!

Jenny and her parents lived in the same building, on 84th Street and West End Avenue, two flights down. But Jenny's cat and turtle, Apricot Jones and Augusta, lived up here.

She had found the turtle last August at camp. Mom and Daddy had been dutifully willing to adopt her, but had wanted her to live in a carton; whereas Aunt Trudl let her have free run of the whole apartment.

Apricot Jones, a creamy white and apricot young cat, had been very small and abandoned, starved and scared, wandering around in January slush and snow under parked cars on West End Avenue when Jenny found her. No sooner had Jenny brought her upstairs than—wouldn't you know—the kitten darted straight into Mom's studio, a place Mom felt very possessive about. And the first thing she did in there was make a puddle under Mom's easel. Luckily Mom always kept paint rags around. Jenny grabbed one. It smelled of turpentine. Quickly she wiped the puddle up.

The next thing Apricot Jones did was inspect Mom's latest painting, which stood propped against the wall to dry. It was a large, semi-abstract seascape. Jenny liked it a lot. It did not show the sky or sea or sand or sun the way they really looked, just shapes and colors; but those were so right, they made you feel all warm and wonderful the way you do at the real beach, as though you were walking by the edge of the water with foam bubbles between your toes, and as though in a second you'd be all cool, plunging in, ducking under waves and riding on top.

11

Apricot Jones stood quite still, gazing at it with wide, blue eyes. She seemed to admire it a lot, even though she probably didn't know what a beach was. Jenny imagined her at a real beach, testing the water with her paw, backing away from it, leaving a trail of dainty paw prints in the sand.

"Hey, no!" she suddenly yelled, as the kitten's right forepaw shot out. Jenny grabbed her away—too late. The damage was done. Where her paw had touched the painting, there was now a gap in the blue-greenness with white canvas showing through, like an unexplainable hole in the sea.

Mom came in. Her look of disapproval at Jenny's being in here without her turned into total dismay when she saw the kitten and what had happened. Her hands flew to her cheeks. She screwed up her face—which was so pretty and young-looking when Mom wasn't all upset. She looked as though she wanted to scream.

Go ahead, scream, Jenny wished, not out loud, only please don't look like that!

"I know I should let you have a pet," Mom said in a tight, clenched voice. "I know it would mean a lot to you. Okay. But if this kitten stays here, I'll be back in no time at all to a pack of Lucky Strikes a day, unfiltered." Even now, her hand groped in her skirt pocket for a cigarette, though there were none in there, though it was over three months ago that she and Jenny's father had given up smoking. "Now let's see if I can rescue this." She lifted the seascape onto the easel and

12

squeezed daubs of blue and green paint onto her palette.

Jenny wanted to stay and watch. She had an idea for a picture of her own—of the slush and snow downstairs, that would somehow show how it had felt, finding Apricot Jones. She wanted very much to try and paint that. But Mom really needed to be in her studio by herself right now, Jenny could tell.

So she took Apricot Jones to Aunt Trudl's. "Anyway, you'll like it better up there," she said into the kitten's pink, shell-like ear. "If you mess things up or do things wrong, Aunt Trudl won't mind. She's more used to that than Mom. And you'll have Mephisto and Murrna for company."

Murrna, a small but fully grown velvet-gray cat with white paws, lay curled on the headboard of Aunt Trudl's bed, watching her pack: old jeans, thick socks, a pair of clumpy hiking shoes—not things she'd wear in London. Also, the suitcase was too small.

"Oh," said Jenny, greatly disappointed, "you're only going to Tannersville."

Aunt Trudl often went there with Silverman, to Silverman's brother's chicken farm. Last spring they had taken Jenny there for a weekend. She had enjoyed it, especially gathering eggs, and milking a cow at the neighboring farm and drinking the milk while it was still warm and frothy.

"Right," said Aunt Trudl. "I thought I'd better

go while you're still here to take care of the cats and Augusta and the plants."

Jenny looked glum.

"You don't mind, do you Jenny?"

"No, I like to." Jenny had a set of keys to the apartment and took care of everything whenever Aunt Trudl was away. "I just mind that you won't—"

"I know. Listen, Jenny, we'll be back Thursday night, late. I'll expect you Friday morning, eight o'clock, for a special farewell breakfast. Very festive. With *Palatschinken,* how does that sound?"

"Good. Mom and Daddy too? Or just me?"

"Just you. They'll be busy with last-minute stuff. Oh, before I forget, tell them they won't need to take a taxi. Silverman's driving us—"

"Us? You mean you might still—?"

"No! I'm coming along to the airport. No farther." Aunt Trudl leaned down to snap the suitcase shut. Jenny was sitting on the bed next to the suitcase. She looked up at her. They both had blue-gray-green eyes. Their eyes met. After two seconds of seeing who could hold out longer, they both started laughing—about looking in each others' faces like this. They looked a lot alike, considering the thirty-seven-year difference in their ages. So naturally Aunt Trudl's face was getting wrinkled and some of her hair was turning gray. But her hair was thick and too curly like Jenny's, and the parts of it that weren't gray yet were the same color blondish-brown as Jenny's. They had the same color and shape eyebrows. Aunt Trudl had a longish nose with a bump in the middle; Jenny's was longish too, and a matching bump was starting to show. They had finely shaped mouths, and pretty big chins with exactly the same little dent in the middle.

Jenny looked over at the mirror that hung above the bureau across from the bed. Seeing her own face and Aunt Trudl's so close together in there, her expression changed from laughing to sad. She thought how far away from each other they would soon be.

She put her arms up and around Aunt Trudl's neck. "I can't help it, I just wish you were coming with us."

"I know you do. But think of it this way: Four would be a crowd."

"No, three's a crowd."

"Not when three's a family."

"But you're Daddy's sister. You're in the family, too."

"Sure, but you know what I mean. This is your chance for the three of you to be really together, with your parents relaxed, not all wrapped up in their work—"

"Mom will drag us to a hundred museums though." Jenny's mother, aside from being a painter, taught art in a high school. "And Daddy has to see clients." Her father was a lawyer.

"That'll take him one morning, the rest of the time he'll be free, he told me so. And there aren't a hundred museums in London. You may get 'dragged' to three or four. And whom are you kidding? You *like* paintings."

That was true. Right this minute, she was looking at one, liking it. Mom had given it to Aunt Trudl a long time ago. It hung next to the mirror. It was of bright orange and deep blue flowers in a shimmering vase that you could tell was crystal.

"I know I do. Just not in museums," said Jenny, and changed the subject back again. "You know the real reason I think you don't want to come with us?"

"No. What?"

"I think you think it's awful there."

"Jenny, that's too silly. I don't think any such thing, and you know it." Aunt Trudl sat down on the bed next to Jenny.

"Then what *do* you think?"

"*It* isn't awful there. *I* was kind of awful, when I was over there. . . ." She turned a little away, to the window, and gazed through it as though that window faced out on long ago instead of just on the brick wall of another part of the apartment building.

"How were you awful? What did you do?"

"Oh, I was homesick and miserable, and jealous. I felt as though I was the only kid in the world separated from her parents. I took everything terribly seriously. And I had awful thoughts that made me feel guilty and ashamed of myself."

"What were they?"

"Don't remind me!"

"But Aunt Trudl, everything would be so different now! You're grown up now—"

"At forty-eight and a half, I'd better be," Aunt Trudl said wryly.

"And you'd be a tourist, not a refugee."

"Look, Jenny, I'm not saying this makes sense. I'm not even asking you to understand. Just accept it: I don't want to go, that's all. Okay?"

"Okay." Jenny bit her right middle fingernail.

Aunt Trudl, unlike most people Jenny knew, did not make a speech about how bad it was to bite one's nails. She felt a person's fingernails were strictly that person's own business. She said, "Silverman'll be here in a few minutes. Meantime, I'll give you some pointers about London: Every morning, stuff your pockets with toast and rolls for the ducks and swans and different kinds of birds, even pelicans, if you're lucky, in the parks. Also, keep an eye out for pictures on the sidewalks. You may see some really good ones—"

"How come they let people draw on sidewalks?"

"I don't know how come. They just do. At least they did, when I was there. And another thing: say 'bags,' if you race with another kid for the front seat on the upper decks of buses."

"How come?"

"Because if there's only one front seat free, whoever says 'bags' first gets it. Don't sit on any lion statues, even the ones that seem to be smiling.

Don't call policemen 'bobbies' to their faces. Try kippers for breakfast. That's herring, smoked instead of pickled, and then heated up in a pan. Or sausages with grilled tomatoes—tom*ahtoes*, as they say. Drink lots of tea, with three lumps of sugar per cup. Pour the milk in first, it tastes better that way, no one knows exactly why. Go to street markets. They have all kinds of good junk and treasures at those. Oh, while I think of it—" She took her pocketbook from the bureau. "You may need a little extra spending money."

"I already have five dollars saved," said Jenny.

"Well, here's five more."

"Thanks!"

"It'll go quickly, you'll see."

"I'll get you a present. What would you like?"

"A sidewalk picture. A smile off a lion statue. Or, how about a jet-black feather freshly plucked from a raven's wing? They have ravens at the Tower, so that shouldn't be too hard."

"Come on, Aunt Trudl, what would you really like?"

"For you to have a fantastic time."

The downstairs bell rang, twice, fast, in a row. "That's Silverman. Two rings is our signal for when he's double parked." She grabbed her suitcase and pocketbook, ran to the hall, buzzed back, and said into the intercom. "I'll be right down."

Murrna wove in and out around her feet, all set to dart out the door after her.

"Don't you dare." Jenny picked her up and held

18

her. "You'd like the chickens in Tannersville, but I don't think they'd like you too much, so you stay right here."

"Thanks, Jenny. There's plenty of milk and cat food. You'll find lettuce, a little raw hamburger, and half a blueberry corn muffin for Augusta. The plants won't need watering till tomorrow." She gave Jenny and Murrna quick kisses on the tops of their heads. " 'Bye. See you Friday morning."

" 'Bye, Aunt Trudl. Have a good time."

Jenny put out enough food and milk for the cats to last them till tomorrow afternoon. She sprinkled fresh cat litter over their box. She put a crisp lettuce leaf and a big piece of blueberry corn muffin under the couch for Augusta. While she was down there, she found Apricot Jones's favorite toy, a miniature plastic beer mug she had once won from a bubblegum machine as a prize.

"Apricot Jones, look what's here!" Jenny rolled it to the cat, the cat rolled it back.

"Now play with it by yourself. I have to go." Jenny took her London guidebook, locked the door, and went home.

Two

"Forty-two and a half more hours till the plane," Jenny figured out the next day, Wednesday, after school, on her way up to Aunt Trudl's.

Apricot Jones came bounding to the door and snuggled around her ankles. Mephisto acknowledged her arrival by blinking one green eye, then continuing his nap in the rocking chair. Murrna was nowhere to be seen. She often went into hiding when Aunt Trudl was away.

Jenny checked under the couch. No Murrna. Only Augusta was down there, asleep. She had eaten the piece of blueberry corn muffin, but not the lettuce. It was wilted. Jenny got her a fresh leaf, with a bit of raw hamburger on it.

She changed the litter box. She washed the cats' dishes. She poured milk in the saucers. She opened two cans of cat food and divided the contents evenly into three bowls.

Apricot Jones and Mephisto—but not Murrna—came racing into the kitchen at the smell.

"Don't you two hog all her food," said Jenny and went to look for Murrna in the living room, the bathroom, the hall, then in the bedroom-study.

It was a hard room to look in because of all the hiding places: under the bed; under the bureau; under the typewriter cover that lay on the floor; inside a desk drawer or file cabinet drawer (Aunt Trudl had left a few open); even on top of the desk somewhere in between all the boxes of manuscripts and stuff; behind the radiator; in the closet. Jenny looked in all those places.

The only other possibility was somewhere on the floor-to-ceiling bookshelves on the wall behind the desk. Careful not to disturb anything, Jenny stood up on the desk. She craned her neck, looked way up, and caught sight of the cat on the highest bookshelf, wedged into the space between the books and the wall.

"Come down from there! Your dinner's waiting! Come on now, be a good Murrrrna," Jenny coaxed.

Murrna stretched and yawned, in no hurry. Leisurely she rose, stepped daintily along behind the books to the end of the shelf. Then she leaped.

She brought something down along with her. Her paws had dislodged it from where it lay. Whirls of dust blew around it as it fell to the floor.

Jenny picked it up.

It was a notebook with a mottled, greenish cardboard cover, with COPYBOOK printed on it in block letters. Underneath that was some writing, very small, in faded ink. Jenny had to hold it close to decipher it:

> This copybook belongs to Gertrude Ehren-
> teil, c/o Sanderson, 17 Stupin Lane, Twiford,
> Surrey, England.

Except for the handwriting being so tiny and the number 7 having a line through it, it looked— every g-loop, i-dot, t-cross, comma, every stroke— exactly like Jenny's own.

She thought, I never knew handwritings run in families, and flopped down on Aunt Trudl's bed and opened the copybook. The pages were yellowed and crackly.

Wow, it's old, she thought and started to read:

July 27, 1938
Mr. Sanderson gave me this copybook, for to improove my English. Mark and Pamela sayd, I had jolly well better improove it fast, or I will get very teazed when I go to school after the hols. Mr. Sanderson sayd I shoud copy new words in here every day, and yuze the words in sentences, and not write anything in German.
NEW WORDS:
1. HOLS. Hols is short for holidays which we shall have til September. That is when their school starts.
2. BAGS. Bags, the lav. Lav is short for

Lavatory. Bags, the last piece of bakon. Bags, I brush Ballou. Ballou is the Sandersons' dog. I always thought it only ment bags for putting things inside! I started having English lessons in Vienna when I was six years old. Now I am eleven and a half, and only now have learnt the most important word in the hole English language, BAGS! Pamela and Mark Sanderson say it all the time. Now that I know it, I will say it too.

3. BLOODY. Bloody is not about blood. It is a word for swaring that grown-ups yuze, but get angry if children yuze it too. Mark sayd, weeding his garden bed is a bloody bore. Mr. Sanderson said that he is bloody spoilt and should not have the priviledje of a garden bed of his own.

4. JOLLY. Jolly does not allways mean happy or funny. Pam sayd I had jolly well better keep hands off Felicity (that is her doll). She ment, I had better keep hands off, or else.

5. PAX. Pam and Mark say that when they are ready to stop fighting. But I am crossing it out because it is not English. It is Latin and means peace.

5. WIZARD. When they say, How wizard, they don't mean a madgician in fairy tales with a beard and cloak on. They mean, how wonderful, or how egciting (I'm not sure I spelt that right).

NEW WORDS:

1. ~~HIPPOCRYT.~~ *I spelt that wrong. It is spelt HYPOCRITE. I looked it up in the dictionary. The dictionary said it is "A false pretender to goodness or piety." I say it is Pam. And Mark.*

2. YEARNING. *I thought that was pronounced like "year." But it's not. It is pronounced like "yer." It means a very great longing. I have such a yearning for my parents. Mutti! Vati!*

I have cried tears down on this page. Mr. Sanderson was right, that I shoud not write anything in German. Not even only those words. Especially not those words. It is good that I am sitting in the larder, and Mark and Pam can't see me. Or they woud call me Crybaby. Boo-hoo to you, they woud say. The larder is a place behind the kitchen. It is smaller than a room but bigger than a cupboard. It smells of potatoes and onions and kittens. Molly has hided her new kittens in here. I think Mrs. Sanderson knows that I come in here sometimes to be by myself. I have also a yearning for the postman. One more hour til he comes. I yearn that he will bring me a letter from my parents. Or from my friend, Upstairs-Lieselotte. She promised she woud write, but I herd her mother say she must not stay friends with Jews.

And if no letter from Upstairs-Lieselotte or my parents, then he will perhapps bring me one from my grandparents. I must write some more new words now.

NEW WORDS:

3. NIROB. Nirob is Mark Sanderson's brown doll with the red velvet trousers. His name yuzed to be Robin. But Mark sais Nirob sounds more Afrikan. Mark is ever so as-chamed of having a doll. But seecretly he likes him.

4. PORCELAIN. Porcelain is almost the same word in German. The heads of Felicity and also of Nirob are made of it. If you drop them they can break. I left my dolls in Vi-enna.

5. SOPPY. Soppy means stupid in a cry-baby way. If Pam calls me that again, I jolly well will swat her.

6. SWAT. To swat is to give a smack.

Below those words the writing became even ti-nier, and had been crossed out. This made it very hard, but not impossible, to read:

~~The Postman has come but he did not bring any letters for me. When I feel so bad like now, I can not even cry, even in the lar-der. This is what I wish for Hitler. That all people to whom he has done harm, even the people whom he killed, coud go to his palass~~

~~in Berchtesgaden or Berlin or wherever he is,~~
~~and do him a torchure. And no matter how~~
~~much the torchures hurt, he coud not dy til~~
~~they were finished. Some of the torchures~~
~~coud be: Hanging up Hitler with iron clothes-~~
~~pegs by his ears. Taring out his mustach hairs~~
~~one by one. The hairs out of his nose holes.~~
~~Then his toe nails. And so fourth. I have~~
~~thought of some torchures too terrible too~~
~~write. I am quite aschamed of this. Does it~~
~~mean that I am eevil? What would Mr. and~~
~~Mrs. Sanderson say if they knew?~~

Jenny had been chewing on the cuticle of her
left index finger. She didn't notice till it started to
hurt. She thought, What if Aunt Trudl knew I was
reading this? She wouldn't like it. I ought to
stop. . . .

She turned the page, though, and saw this picture:

That's weird, Jenny thought. Her arms broke out in goose bumps. The hair on her arms stood on end. She looked at the picture a long time.

Underneath it was written, *Mariedl's Tail.*

She thought for a moment that Mariedl would turn out to be the name of the guy with the horns and wings and tail. Then she thought, No. Because he was the Devil. Mariedl would be somebody else. And *tail* was misspelled. Trudl must have meant tale, like a story.

MARIEDL'S TAIL

While the Devil was falling out of Heaven down into Hell, a great, tremenduss emerald that he had in his forhead fell out. Some angels came flying, and they cawt the emerald in their arms. Now all the emeralds that are in the hole world come from that one. And so all emeralds in the world have magic. Some of their magic is for bad, becauze of the Devil. Some is for good, becauze of the angels. You cannot tell just by looking which kind which emeralds have.

Then,

WARNING!

it said on the next page, in suddenly bold, enormous letters.

This copybook is deeply seecret. Whosoever disobeys this warning and reads on, shall be my bitter ennemie. And I bloody well curse you forever.

28

To this was affixed, with ceremonious curlicues and flourishes, the signature,

Underneath appeared this drawing:

Then came still another warning in spidery, menacing letters:

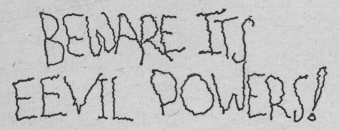

Jenny could not bear to stop reading now. Yet, after such a warning, how did she dare read on? She felt torn. She kept her eyes a while longer on

that eerie page with the different printing, script, and lettering, and especially on the picture of the ring.

Then she forced herself to look away. She closed the copybook. She climbed on the desk and stuck it back up on the shelf.

Three

As soon as Jenny got home Nancy Saradjan called. They were best friends. They told each other everything. Usually they talked on the phone until one of their mothers made them get off.

"Hey, guess who just called me." said Nancy. "S. Susan Morris! Isn't that amazing?"

The S stood for Sexy. Susan was the leader of a bunch of cliquey girls in their class who bragged about all the boy-girl parties they went to and acted superior to people who didn't go to parties like that. Susan already wore a brassiere she kept tugging at, so everybody would be sure to notice. She carried a lipstick in her pocketbook, and she had a photograph in her wallet of her cousin Eddie, who was already in college. She was always showing it to kids. Yes, he looked a lot like Robert Redford, she wanted everyone to say, even though he didn't.

"She asked me the math homework," Nancy went on. "Guess what else though. She invited me over to her house tomorrow. Hey, Jenny—?"

"What?"

ı was just checking if you're still there. You haven't said a word. Are you mad, or something?"

"Uh uh."

"Well, anyway I said No, because you're coming to my house. You are, aren't you? It's the last day we'll see each other."

"Yes, I'll come over."

"You already sound about a million miles away. Like you're already up in the airplane. Or already in London. Boy, do I wish I was going!"

"I have to get off the phone now, Nancy."

"How come? We haven't talked a minute yet."

"I just have to." Jenny thought, Because if I don't, I'll tell her about the copybook. And I shouldn't. I shouldn't tell anyone.

"Okay, 'bye." They hung up.

At dinner Jenny asked her father, "Are you eleven or twelve years younger than Aunt Trudl?"

"Almost thirteen. Why?"

"I was just thinking. . . . Didn't it feel strange when you were little, having a sister that much older than you, and who was born in a whole other country and had a whole bunch of things happen to her, like being a refugee and all that, before you even knew her?"

"It did feel strange, yes. I could never get her to talk much about those things. Does she, to you?"

"Uh uh. Daddy, who do you think was the worst person in the history of the world? D'you think it was Hitler?"

"Well, there were some maniacs in ancient

times who threw people off cliffs, or fed them to lions for fun—"

"And Mussolini, and Goering, and Himmler," said Mom.

"And Goebbels, and Eichmann, and Stalin, who was really no pussycat either. But, yes, I'd go out on a limb and say Hitler was the worst. Are you studying World War Two in social studies?"

"No."

"Then what makes you ask?"

"I was just thinking. . . ."

. . . About the copybook. She went on thinking about it while helping with the dishes, while watching the news, while trying to finish *A Kids' Guide to London,* while taking a bath and getting into pajamas, an old pair she wasn't planning to take along. It stayed in her mind so persistently, she wished that she hadn't found it. At the same time she wished, even more, that she could read the rest.

She felt so uneasy about the whole thing, she did something she hadn't done in a long time: She took Esther and April, both her dolls, to bed with her.

Their presence didn't help, though. When she closed her eyes, she saw the copybook handwriting so maddeningly clearly on the insides of her eyelids, she could *almost, almost* make the words out.

And then she dreamed such weird, foreboding dreams, she was glad when the night was over.

Thursday after school she said, "I'm really sorry, Nancy. But I can't come over."

"But you *said*—"

"I know. It's just, I have all these things I have to do."

"Like what?"

"I have to sort out all my stuff and decide what I'm taking. Then I have to go to Rexall's and get a new toothbrush. And Mom gave me a whole list of things to get for her and Daddy."

"I could go with you."

"I guess so—"

"You don't want me to," Nancy looked hurt.

"I do so." Jenny felt bad.

"It's okay, I'll see you when you get back from your trip. I hope you have a nice time," said Nancy very formally.

"I'll call you tonight. And I'll write to you," Jenny promised.

Buying the things at the drugstore took less than ten minutes. It took another fifteen to lay out on her bed the things she would pack: clothes; new toothbrush; toothpaste; hairbrush; comb; rubber bands and barrettes for different ways to wear her hair; a sketch pad and pastels Mom had gotten her; the guidebook to London; a couple of paperbacks; and April and Esther, although she was still not sure which of them she would take.

Then she went up to Aunt Trudl's.

It was very peaceful there. Mephisto lay on the couch like a shaggy, black, orange-flecked twenty-fourth scatter cushion. The window with all the plants on it looked like a bright jungle. The afternoon sun shone in.

Apricot Jones meowed around Jenny's legs. Jenny picked her up and petted her. Then she changed the litter box, washed the saucers and bowls, found Augusta, fed her.

Then, starting to water the plants, she noticed a new purple bud and blossom on one, and thought, Oh, good, the African violet's in bloom. African . . . "Afrikan" . . . She put the watering can down and thought about Nirob, the "Afrikan" doll in the copybook. . . .

Once, when she and Daddy were taking a walk down on Bleecker Street, she had seen a really handsome, dark brown boy doll with alive-looking eyes and a turban on his head in the window of an antiques store. They'd gone in, and Daddy asked how much he cost. Too much. Jenny had wished they could have bought him.

She wondered if Nirob whom Mark Sanderson was so "aschamed" of, but "seecretly" liked, had looked anything like that doll in the store.

What other "seecrets" were in the copybook?

She tried to smile at all the misspellings, but she couldn't. The muscles of her face were tense. Her whole body was tense, from keeping a tight hold on herself, trying to keep from admitting how very badly she wanted to go and get the copybook down.

She started watering again, and over-watered a spider plant. The window sill and floor got wet. But she did not go for a rag. If she left the living room now, she knew where she'd end up.

She hung her head down and shook it, the way the gym teacher had showed her class, to shake the tension loose. And, Jenny thought, to shake away the desire. Her hair flew wildly around her face. She did not get less tense, only dizzy. And the desire grew stronger.

I'm not the kind of person who pokes into other people's secrets, she reminded herself. And she resolved, I will not read the copybook.

The sun shining on Mephisto's face woke him. He yawned, showing his sharp teeth and the pink ridges inside his mouth. He leaped down off the couch and ambled to the rocking chair, crossing the room directly in front of where Jenny stood.

It's a good thing he has orange flecks, so he doesn't count as a black cat, she caught herself thinking. How dumb! I've known him all my life, he's never brought me bad luck. I don't even believe in bad luck, or curses, or any superstitious things like that. Even so, *I still won't read Aunt Trudl's copybook*. Because if it were mine, *I* wouldn't want anybody to read it. There, I'm glad that's settled. Now I'll feed the cats. I wonder where Murrna's hiding today? "Murrna, Murrna," she called. I guess I'd better go find her. . . .

And she went into the bedroom-study.

No sooner in there than she stood up on the desk and took the copybook down.

She plunged onto the bed with it. It fell open— by chance!—to the page with the warning. She averted her eyes, turned quickly to the next page, and read.

Four

July 30

*It is the middle of the night. Pamela snores.
I have my bed lamp on. It gives not much
light. If Pam wakes up and asks me what I am
doing, I shall say, writing to my parents, she
can't kriticize me for that.*

*But my parents have too much to worry
about: me away. The Nazis in Austria. So
many Jews going to prison. And when will
our quota numbers come up? (Quota numbers are for going to America. Untill your
quota number comes up, America won't let
you in.)*

*The bad thoughts I am having woud make
my parents only worry more. I cannot write
them in letters. I cannot tell them to any
body. So I am writing them down into here,
instead of new words. My English is anyway
improoving. But other parts of me are getting
worse:*

38

1. My fingernails. I have been biting them badly.

Me too, thought Jenny, but did not take the one she was chewing on out of her mouth.

2. My ungratitude. Mark and Pam's parents were kind to take in a refugee child. They coud not know they woud get one with eevil thoughts and who seldom smiles. But I am so homesick and hate it so much here!

REASONS WHY I HATE IT HERE:

1. Becauze Pamela is such a hippoc—

July 31

Then Pam woke up and I had to stop. Now it is day. She has gone to the stable. Mark has gone to the river to catsch frogs. I am in the larder and I have time to write down all the reazons:

1. Becauze she is a hippocrite.

2. Becauze Mark is also one.

3. Becauze they teaze me very much.

4. And I have not such a good sense of humour. I shoud laugh and say, I don't care, instead of let them see me cry.

5. And I wisch awful things woud happen to Mark and Pam.

6. If the house shoud catsch on fire, and Mr. and Mrs. Sanderson had only time to save two children, they woud save Mark and Pam, and I woud dy.

7. I have not got any dolls.

HOW PAM IS A HIPPOCRITE: *At night she thinks I don't see her and she gets out of bed. She takes Felicity off the chest of drawers. She always sais she does not play with dolls any more, becauze she is allready so grown up. A hippocrite is a person who sais one thing, then does the very oppozit. She takes Felicity into her bed. In the morning Felicity is back on the chest as if she had sat there the hole night long.*

THE REASON I LEFT MY DOLLS IN VIENNA: *To proove how grown-up I am. If I had taken them with me, I woud have seemed like a baby. And my mother woud have minded still more, that she was sending me away. Therefor I did not even take my smallest doll, Resi, though I coud have put her in the pockett of the white dress, I mean, frock, with the red poppies I had on that day.*

MY DRESS WITH THE POPPIES: *My mother has such a dress. Some material was left over from it, so Mariedl sewed a dress just like it for me. Mariedl was the housekeeper of my grandparents. The dress has sleeves like wings, not puffed sleeves which are babyish. It is not so short like my other dresses, and does not just hang, but goes in at the waste.*

The Children's Transport lady pinned a big

label on it, with my name and where I was going, like on a parcel. I thought the label spoilt it. But without the label, Mr. Sanderson woud not have known who I am.

He works in a busyness in London. Therefor only he came, not the hole Sanderson family, to get me from the Children's Transport place. And he said, "What a pretty frock you have on." He was very nice to me.

We took a train from another train station than the one where the Children's Transport train arrived. And after the train we took a bus to Twiford. All the time Mr. Sanderson told me how egsited Pamela and Mark were that I was coming to stay, and how much I woud like them. He said we woud be jolly good friends.

When the bus came into Twiford, they and their mother waited in front of the pub where the bus woud stop. The pub is called the Stirrup Cup. Mrs. Sanderson looked like I always thought an English country lady woud look: tall and thin with a strict face and hair in a net, and galosches on although it did not rain. The boy had a school cap on. He was also tall, with thin, long legs and nobby knees. He held orange flowers. "Those are naturshums, from Markie's own garden bed," Mr. Sanderson sayd. "He has brought them for you." I sayd, "That was nice of him."

Pamela wore riding clothes and a round

black hat. She has long, thick red-brown hair. That day she wore it in one plait. It hung down her back. Later I saw how pretty is her face, with thin eyebrows, not bushy like mine, and eyes that match her hair and fair skin and a strait thin nose. She already has bosoms. I thought it must be wonderful to horseback ride. I douted I ever coud.

Suddenly I did not like my frock with the poppies anymore. I did not feel grown up in it, only dressed up, like for a children's party. And foreign. And foolish. I wisched, I wisched this Pamela woud like me. But I was sure she woud not.

I did not wear my poppy frock again until today. This morning when I put it on, I skweezed shut my eyes and wisched to God (in Whom I don't believe) that when I put my hand into the pockett, Resi woud be there. If she was, I promissed to believe in God. Surprise: Resi was not in the pockett.

WHEN I FIRST STARTED HATING PAM AND MARK: *The very first day. They shook hands and said, "How do you do," ever so nicely. But already, when the parents were not looking, Mark made teazing faces at me.*

I did like the house. The bottom part is built of stone. The top part is wooden, and painted white. The windows have dark green shutters. The front door is shiny black. And there is a garden.

Pamela showed me her room, where I woud sleep. I knew she was not glad that she woud have to share it.

Then she and Mark showed me the garden and Ballou. Ballou is an Irish setter dog. Mark said, "It's a pity he's not a poodle."

He wanted me to ask, "Why?" so I did.

"Because poodle rhymes with Trudl, ha, ha."

"And noodle," said Pam.

"And strudel," said Mark. "Strudel is a Viennese sweet, isn't it? And you like it, don't you, Trudl?"

"Of course she does." Pam picked up some earth and held it out to me. "Here, Trudl, have some noodle strudel!"

I knew that I shoud laugh and say, "No thanks," as though I did not mind. But I sayd, "There is no such dish in Vienna as noodle strudel. If there were I woud not like it. You can call me Gertrude, if you woud rather."

"Dirtrude?" asked Mark.

By then I cryed. And they called me crybaby.

Then Pam said, "Pax. We were only teazing." But I thought it was only becauze their mother was coming.

August 2

Pam goes riding every other day. She is riding now. Mark is weeding his garden bed. Mr.

Sanderson has given me also one. In autum I will put bulbs in. Bulbs are like onions. But in spring, out of the bulbs will grow daffodils and tulips and such. Mr. Sanderson sayd perhapps by spring I will allready be in America with my parents. Then he showed me which are weeds. Some of them have blossoms too, so it is not eazy to tell them from the flowers.

The thing I wisch most in the world is that what he sayd about spring woud come true. The thing I wisch next most is that I had a doll. I woud also like to horseback ride.

August 3

I feel sorry for Felicity. Felicity means happiness. But I dout she coud be happy with Pam for a mother. Becauze Pam trys not to play with her at all any more. How dreadful it woud be, if this coud happen with real mothers! Pam has not taken Felicity into her bed this hole week. Felicity just sits on the chest of drawers and is no good to any body, and no body is any good to her.

So I have decided to make up a story about her. In the story her name will be Felicity-Emma. I will write the story in here:

FELICITY-EMMA

She wants to belong to me. She wants to so much, it is she who is making me make up this story. It is she who has put the idea of it

44

*into my mind. (This is so strange, it makes me
shiver. Woudn't it be wizard if it were really
so?!)*

*Felicity's mouth is a little bit open. Her eyes
are green. (I never saw a doll with green eyes
before.) They are also very keen eyes, for she
has seen my ring. And now I have to inter-
rupt the story about Felicity-Emma to tell
about my ring:*

MY RING
*My ring is golden with an emerald. The
emerald is shaped like a tiny egg. It is bright
green.*

*This ring belonged to my great-
grandmother. My great-grandmother gave it
to my grandmother when my grandmother
turned eighteen. My grandmother gave it to
my mother when my mother turned eighteen.
And I was suppozed to get it on my eigh-
teenth birthday. But my mother sayd I shoud
not have to wait that long. Becauze I was
doing such a grown-up thing, going away to
England without my parents. She sayd that I
shuud already have the ring, even though I
will be twolve on my birthday, the fifth of
November. So she gave it to me at the train station. I always looked so forward to getting it!
But now I did not want it so very much as I
always thought I woud. I almost sayd, No! I
did not want to do the grown-up thing. I did*

not want to go to England without them. I did not think Hitler coud be as bad as having to go away was bad. I wanted to get as heavy as the elephant in Schönbrunn (that is the zoo). Then nobody coud lift me up the steps into the train wagon. I wanted to cry, "Mutti and Vati, don't make me get on!" But I got on the train with many other Viennese Jewish children. My parents waived to me. I waived to them. The ring is on my middle finger. It is too big to wear on my ring finger. It looks not so good on my hand becauze my nails are bitten. (That is a German word, too: Bitten. It means, to beg.) Every time I bite my nails I think it is the last time and from now on I will not bite them any more.

One night when I was still at home I asked my mother what she thought about Mariedl's story about the emerald falling out of the Devil's forhead. My mother sayd, Mariedl uzed to tell her also such stories when she was little. And she laughed. And she sayd, "It's Larifari." I said, "What does that mean?" And she said, "It means Blödsinn." That sounds like blood, and sin. But it means only, silly nonsense.

But in my story about the doll, all that about the emerald is not such Larifari and not such Blödsinn either.

FELICITY-EMMA AGAIN

I am naming her also Emma, in honour of the emerald. Becauze she saw it on my finger with her keen green eyes. And becauze she knew it had magic powers, and thought the good ones coud make her be alive.

Now comes a part of the story that is harder to make myself believe than the magic parts: Pamela gives me Felicity-Emma. Not becauze she thinks I am such a baby who needs to have a doll. Just becauze she wants to.

Now comes a seecret wonder about Felicity-Emma: She breathes air in and out. She has thoughts. She has wisches. When I touch her she feels it. She can do everything.

Now she comes into my bed. And we go on an adventure.

Moonlight shines into the room. I catsch some with my emerald. I spread it all over Felicity-Emma and me. It makes us invisibel.

We go out of here. We go down the stairs and outside. No body can see us.

"Ballou, Ballou!" I call in an unhearabel voice that only a dog can hear. Ballou comes running.

We go to the stable. It is not so near. I do not know egsactly where it is. But we run like the wind. And soon we are there.

"Midnight, Midnight!" I call. That is the name of the horse Pamela rides. I hear snort-

ing and hoof sounds on the ground. Mid-
night's stall is shut. It opens. She has opened
it with her nose, perhapps. Or, perhapps, I,
with my moonlight-voice.

Midnight comes out.

"Oh what a beauty, how proud she is," says
Felicity-Emma.

Midnight holds her head high. She is
blacker than the real midnight around us. She
has one star, like the horse Black Beauty, on
her forhead. Only the horse in that book was
a stallion. This one is a she-horse, a mare.

She winnies to us very friendlily. We get
on. I have never been on horseback before.
But I can ride perfectly!

Midnight has no saddel. She has reins
though, and I guide her. I have no breeches
on, only my nightdress. That is all right, that
is fine. Her bare back feels like velvet. Her
mane and tale feel like silk.

We wade across the shallow ford with
moonlight on it. We ride through weeds, we
canter and galopp through open fields. We
jump over hedjes. I am not afraid. Nor is
Felicity-Emma. We do not fall. Ballou runs
and runs along side, and he yips and he yips
for joy.

August 5

Last night, in the middle of the night I got
up to fetch Felicity-Emma into bed, and Pam
awoke. So I sayd, "I'm just going to the lav."

A CERTAIN MAGIC

Pam thinks it is very babyish to have to go to the lav at night (except when she has to).

August 7
I feel so dreadful, I cannot go on with the story of Felicity-Emma. Something dreadful and bad has happened:

"Yeeeow!" loud and fierce, came from the living room. Something bad's happening in there too, right now, Jenny thought. I'd better go see.

She went in there. Apricot Jones flashed across the window sill, Mephisto pursuing. He knocked over a philodendron plant. It clunked to the floor.

Apricot Jones fled behind the curtain.

Mephisto faced Jenny, glaring, as if to say, "I'm the lord of this window sill."

Any other time she would have scolded him or given him a smack. Now she didn't even take the time to make him get down from there. Hurriedly she stuffed the plant back in the pot. It had only chipped, not broken.

The cuckoo cuckooed five o'clock. It's late, I should start getting the cats' dinner, she thought. But instead she ran into the other room, back to the copybook, and read on.

Five

I feel so dreadful, I cannot go on with the story of Felicity-Emma. Something dreadful and bad has happened:

Yesterday a friend of Mark's, Simon Dolger, came to tea. Mark was afraid Simon woud make fun of him for owning a doll. He came in our room in the morning and sayd, "I'm tired of Nirob. D'you want him, Pam?"

She shrugged.

Nirob is darker than toffee, and lighter than coffee beans. His eyes look very kind. His hair is painted on, but it looks almost real. He has red velvet trousers and a fine white shirt.

"I want him!" I yearned to shout. I sayd, "I'll swap you something of mine if you'll let me have Nirob."

"You can't have him," Pam said. "He's an airloom." I did not know what that was.

"What'll you swap, Trudi?" Mark asked.

50

He must have thought, What can she possibly have worth swapping?

"This." I showed him my ring.

"Hm. But what woud I do with a girl's ring?"

"Magic," I said.

He and Pam looked at each other as if I was dotty. Mark asked, "What did you say?"

"I said, you could do magic with it. This emerald has magic."

"Oh, rot," said Pam.

"Not rot. Listen: When the Devil fell out of Heaven—" and I told them Mariedl's hole tale.

They listened quite hard.

But when I was done Pam said, "It is rot. Mark, you'd be a fool to swap Nirob for her ring. At any rate, our parents wouldn't let you. Besides, having a girl's ring is as bad as having a doll."

"You woudn't have to wear it," I said. "You coud yuze it just to make things happen."

"Why don't you make things happen, then?" Pam asked me. I thought she ment, Why didn't I make myself beautiful with suddenly bosoms and hair as long as hers? Why didn't I suddenly speak English without a foreign accent? And why didn't I make our quota numbers for America come up right away?

51

"*I do make things happen,*" *I said, hating her.* "*Things that you can't know.*"

"*I see,*" *said she superiorly.* "*Then you don't really want to part with your ring, do you, Trudl? Listen, Markie: I'll swap you my goldfish. The goldfish bowl, too.*"

I hate you so much! I thought. I said, "*I thought you're too grown up for dolls.*"

"*So I am. I only want Nirob for an ornament, to sit on my pillow by day. D'you mind?*"

Yes, I minded a thousand times a thousand times!

"*Well, Markie, what do you say?*"

"*Markie*" *said,* "*Right.*" *He gave Nirob with the kind eyes to unkind hippocrite Pam. In return he took her silly old goldfish.*

I bit my thumbnail down to the flesh. I thought, I'll make you sorry!

For tea there were thin salmon paste and watercress sandwiches. And there were currant tarts. But I coud eat none.

Afterwards, Pam, Mark, and Simon went down to the river. Mrs. Sanderson sayd, "*Trudl, dear, why don't you go along?*"

Becauze I had other things to do! I went into Mark's room. I took off my ring. I held it between my thumb and forfinger. I shined the emerald straight at the goldfish's eye. And I sayd very frighteningly,

A CERTAIN MAGIC

Silly old fish, so gold and red,
May this emerald make you dead!

Apricot Jones leaped onto the bed. She curled up next to Jenny and stuck her face out to be stroked under the chin. Jenny stroked her there. The touch of cool, smooth fur made her realize how clammy with sweat her fingers had gotten. "Good Apricot Jones," she tried to say, grateful for her company, but had trouble getting the words out. In her throat was a hard, choking lump of shame at herself for having read this far. She swallowed. The lump remained, the shame remained. And she read on:

Monday, August 8
I am in the larder. Molly is asleep. Her kittens are fighting for turns to suck milk from her. She must be very tired to sleep through that. I am quite tired too. Much happened yesterday:
"The goldfish died!" Mark woke us up at six o'clock and told us. "He was too old, no fair! I want Nirob back."
"'Tisn't my fault your goldfish died," sayd Pam.
It was my fault. My heart knocked, bump, bump. My ring flashed up at me like an eevil beast's eye. I twisted it half way about so I woud not see the emerald. I closed my fist over it.

53

"Shall we have a burial?" asked Pamela.

Mark nodded his head. "And give me back Nirob."

"Oh, all right." Pamela gave back the doll.

Then we went out in our nightclothes and buried the fish in Mark's garden bed.

I picked a red rose from the rose bed. A thorn stuck into my thumb. My thumb bled. I thought, Good, let it. I stuck the rose on the fish's graive. Then we sang, "All Things Bright and Beautiful," the first stanza:

> *All things bright and beautiful,*
> *All creatures great and small,*
> *All things wise and wonderful,*
> *The Lord God made them all.*

I already wrote in here that I don't believe in God. And if I did believe, I woud still not believe that He is a lord. But I like this hymn the best of all I have heard in church. I really love this hymn. I do go to church on Sundays here, although I am Jewish. Mr. and Mrs. Sanderson say that is all right.

At any rate, while we were singing round the graive, Mrs. Sanderson came out of the house, with her mackintosh on over her nightdress. "What on earth are you three doing out here at this hour?"

"We're burying the goldfish. He dyed." Mark showed her the graive.

"*Oh dear. The poor thing. He was frightfully old, wasn't he?*"

Mark nodded.

"*A year and two months,*" *sayd Pam.*

I burst into tears.

"*Why shoud you bawl?*" *Pam asked.* "*He wasn't anything to you.*"

Mrs. Sanderson thought I was crying becauze of my thumb. She took out her pockett handkerchief and tied it round my thumb. "*There, is that better?*"

I still coud not stop.

"*She's just a cry-baby,*" *sayd Mark.*

"*That's not a kind name to call anyone, is it?*" *sayd Mrs. Sanderson. She sent Pam and Mark inside. She put her arm round me. Her face looked not so strict now. Her hair was not in a net. It hung down loose to where I coud smell it.* "*Trudl, shall we have a little chat?*" *She spread her mack out on the grass beside Mark's garden bed.* "*Come, let's sit here. Now then, I wish you'd tell me what it is that's making you so unhappy.*"

Her hair smelt like my mother's hair. The grass was wet. But she did not have galosches on. I told her that I'd wanted to swap my ring for Nirob. But that Mark had swapped Nirob for the fish. And that I'd wished the goldfish dead with my ring. And about the emerald's magic.

Mrs. Sanderson took my hand. She made a

"tsk tsk" sound at my nails, how awfully bitten they were. I was so aschamed. Then she turned my ring about so she coud see the emerald. "It's beautiful," she sayd. "You shoud be very proud of it. But of course it isn't the least bit magical, Trudl. That's only a legend. And the goldfish died of perfectly natural causes. You mustn't blame the emerald one bit."

Then we went inside. She made us early tea. And she told about Nirob. The grandfather of Pam and Mark travelled in Afrika when he was quite a young man, and there he bought Nirob, as a present for his wife, but really for himself, to remind himself of there. And when Mark and Pam's father was a small boy, he played with Nirob. "So you see, Trudl, Nirob has been in the family for a long time. Almost as long as your ring has been in your family." Then she sayd, too, that Nirob is an airloom.

That made me think of the seecret about Felicity-Emma, that she breathes air in and out. I asked Mrs. Sanderson, what is an airloom?

"It's something you inherit, as an heir." Mrs. Sanderson spelt it, "H-e-i-r-l-o-o-m. The h is silent." She looked at me. "As you are, very often." And she asked me, "Woud it help if I told Mark to let you play with Nirob as much as you like while you're staying with us?"

"No, please don't do that! It woud only make things worse.

So she promised she woud not. She looked sad. She sayd she knew that it was hard to be not with my own parents, and that Mark and Pam were often beastly to me.

I tried to say No, they weren't, but I coud not.

"Underneath the teazing, they do like you, you know," Mrs. Sanderson sayd.

I sayd, "I know." I wanted to make her feel not so sad for me. I wanted to tell that if I was home in Vienna and an English girl staid with us who acted foreign and spoke not so good German I would teaze her, as Pam and Mark do me. Only that made me think of my room at home and my doll Resi on my pillow, and I coud not talk for fear she woud see me cry.

She put her hand on my cheek. For half a second. Her hand felt soft. "Never mind!" she sayd, and her sad look went suddenly away. "I know something that'll take your mind off it all for a bit. Today, right after church, you'll see!"

I asked what woud I see.

"A surprize. A great treat."

But first we went to church. And I felt bad again. Becauze all the other people there be-

*lieve in God, only not me. And becauze "All
Things Bright and Beautiful" was not one of
the hymns for singing. And becauze the fish
was all smelly and dead in the ground, and
worms were allready perhapps eating his
body.*

*But the surprize treat was, the vicar, who is
a friend of the Sandersons, lent us his motor
car, and Mr. Sanderson drove the hole family
straight from church into London, and we
went straight to Regent's Park Zoo.*

*It has kangaroos, panda bears, an okapi, a
gnu (the g is silent), and ostriches that I have
never seen before. It is even a bigger zoo than
Schönbrunn. Oh, it was wizard, wizard! Pam
and Mark and I loved it. And for once the
three of us got on.*

*We had candy floss. That is pink and sticky
on a stick. At first it looks like a tremenduss
lot, but is only air and sugar. "Skrumpshus,"
sayd Pam. I know I spelt it wrong. It means
the same as delicious. Then we had ice cream
and peanuts. And Pam ate some animal food
you can buy there. She sayd if it was good
enough for the animals, it was good enough
for her.*

*Mr. and Mrs. Sanderson bought us presents
from a peddler's cart:*

A hoop for Pam.

*A huge balloon in the shape of a Mickey
Mouse head for Mark.*

A rubber monkey on a string between two wooden sticks for me. When you moved the sticks about he coud do leaps and somersaults. If you moved the sticks a certain way and sang "Doing the Lambeth Walk," he coud dance that dance.

On the ride home, Mark's Mickey Mouse balloon flew out the window of the motor car. We saw it float over the chimney pots. It went higher than some pidjeons. Then we could not see it anymore.

Mark cried about it.

Becauze we were almost friends now, I did not call him cry-baby.

"I say, Trudl, can I hold your monkey for a sec?" he asked.

So I let him. He made the monkey do somersaults forwards and backwards. "I say, Trudl," he sayd, but then did not say anything.

"What, Mark?"

"Woud you swap me the monkey—?"

"What for?" I asked. I knew already now that Nirob was an air heirloom, and coud not belong to me. Still, I held my breath. I touched my emerald with the fingers of my other hand. Under my breath, so nobody coud hear, I begged it, "Let him swap me Nirob."

And he wanted to! "You can have Nirob till

*you go to America," he said. "All right,
Trudl?"*

"All right!"

*We shook hands. Under my breath I
thanked the emerald from—as people say in
books—the bottom of my heart.*

*It was allready dark when we came back to
Twiford.*

*To get in the house we had to walk past
Mark's garden bed, past the fish's graive. For
a second I could almost not breath, becauze I
had this thought: The emerald got me Nirob.
It does, it must have magic. . . .*

*"What's the matter, Trudl? Aren't you
glad?" Mark asked when he gave me Nirob.
I was not as glad as I had thought I'd be.*

*And I still cannot be so glad. Not untill I
make quite sure that the emerald will never
do bad things again. I do not yet know how I
can make sure of this. But after writing down
into this seecret copybook all that has happened, I am starting to know. At least I have
an idea.*

I have an idea what *I* should do: stop reading,
right now, Jenny thought.

But she could not. Not even when the telephone
on top of the headboard started ringing.

She let it ring, two times, five times, six . . . She
felt as though the age of tele-video-phones was already now, not off in the future; as though, if she

picked up the receiver, whoever was calling would be able to see the copybook on the bed, would know at once that it was secret and that she was reading it.

The phone rang on, seven times, eight times, nine. At last it stopped.

Jenny went on reading.

> When Pam and I were in bed, both her parents came in to say Good night. I had Nirob in my bed.
>
> "I see you've got Nirob," sayd Mrs. Sanderson. "I'm so glad."
>
> "Mark swapped him to me for my monkey. For as long as I'm in Twiford," I egsplained.
>
> "That was jolly decent of him," sayd Mr. Sanderson.
>
> "I say, Trudl," sayd Pam, "you can have Felicity too. I'll let you keep her till you go to America."
>
> I coud not believe it. I egspected she only sayd it so her father woud say, "Jolly decent of you, Pam." I egspected she woud take it back as soon as they left the room.
>
> But when they left the room, she sayd, "Go on, Trudl, take her."
>
> I thought, My emerald is doing this! It's reading the wishes in my mind and making them come true!
>
> I took Felicity-Emma down from the chest of drawers and brought her in my bed. I sayd,

"Thanks, Pam. Thanks ever so much."

"That's quite all right," she sayd.

But that isn't like her, I thought. And I felt not so quite all right. Of course I was glad about the dolls. But I felt—I don't know the word in English for it, a word for feeling frightened and egcited both together becauze something strainge you cannot understand is happening. And I coud not fall asleep.

I thought Pam was sleeping. But then she made a strainge noise. It was a—I don't know the word for that either. It is when what you have eaten comes back up into your throat and tastes there bitter and bad. She growned, "Oh, ooh! I feel gastly!"

Now I got frightened still more. I thought, What if the emerald knows an awful, awful wish that I didn't even myself know I wished? And what if Pam should d—? I won't write that. "What's the matter?" I asked.

"Ooo, oooh, I've got a gastly tummy ache!"

"I'll fetch your mother."

"No, don't!" Then she started to be sick. She ran to the lav. I did too. She finished being sick there. I held her forhead like my mother held mine when I did that. Some vomit got on my foot.

Then we went back to bed. Pam sayd, "Now I'm better."

I was so glad! I asked, "But why didn't you want me to fetch your mother?"

"*Becauze she mustn't know I've been sick. Please, Trudl, don't tell her. I'll do anything if you promiss me you won't.*"

"*Really? Anything?*"

"*Yes.*"

I held my breath. I didn't know myself yet what I was going to ask: "*Will you give me Felicity-Em—um (I nearly gave her seecret name away!)—for good?*"

"*You mean to take with you to America?*"

"*Yes,*" I sayd, surprized myself.

And Pam sayd, "*Yes, all right, I promiss. Now you promiss you won't tell.*"

So I promissed.

Then she told me she had to be at the stable at nine in the morning, and they woud let her jump the cross rail, that is a kind of jump, on Midnight's back. She sayd, "*I've wanted to do that for ever so long, I'm simply dying to. But if my mother finds out that I was sick, she'll make me stay home, she won't let me go.*"

I sayd, "*Don't worry, she won't find out.*" Then we sayd Good night. But it was a bad night and I had frightful nightmaires.

Six

Still August 8

I woke up this morning and Pam was not in her bed. Now I was dredfully afraid. What if something happened bad, while I'd been asleep?

But she was only in the lav. She came back and she was fine. She was already dressed. She looked like an advertizement in the Picture Post for riding costumes.

After breakfast I sayd, "Good luck with the cross rail."

"Thanks." And she asked me, "D'you want to come and watch me?"

Yes, I wanted to, and to see the real Midnight! But then I thought, what if the emerald's eevil makes Midnight fall and throw Pam off? I sayd, "No, I can't."

I coud not stand having these awful thoughts and being frightened anymore.

Pam left for the stable. Mark was off to the Dolgers.

*I went back to Pam's and my room. I shut
the door. I wisched that I coud lock it, too.*

*I pulled out my trunk from under my bed.
It has only my clothes for winter in it, and my
manicure set. That is an elegant thing in a red
lether kase with zipper all around. Vati gave
it to me for my last birthday. He thought having such a thing would make me stop biting
my nails.*

*I took it out. I took out the nail file that
has—that had, rather—a quite sharp point.
And I started to dig out the emerald from my
ring.*

I dugg and dugg.

The emerald budjed not.

*Hurry up, I wisched, come loose now, be-
fore Pam gets to the stable, before she mounts
Midnight . . .*

*I wedjed the tip of the file in between the
gold and the stone. I feared the tip would
break off. I twisted and dugg. And I prayed:
to the Jewish God my grandparents in Vienna
believe in, and to the Christian God the people in the Twiford church believe in. They
were Both the Same to me, since I did not believe in Either. "God, God, let this emerald
come loose!"*

*It still budjed not. Then the file tip did
break off. I did not care. What do I need the
file for? I perhapps will always bite my nails.*

*I only cared about this: The emerald loos-
ened at last. At last I got it out!*

*I klutched it in my fist. Now what should I
do? I only knew it must not be where it coud
ever do eevil things again with its magic.*

*I went to the window. What if I chucked it
out? It would land on the square lawn in the
middle of the garden, in the thick green grass.
No one woud ever find it. Good, then it could
no more do harm . . . Well, that was what I
wanted, then what for was I crying, Boo hoo
to me? Becauze there it woud ly, and I'd
never see it again.*

*All around the lawn are flower beds. I
opened the window. The hinje made a
squeak. Mrs. Sanderson was squatting in the
flower bed under the window, putting pe-
toonias in the ground. She looked up when
the hinje squeaked and she waived to me.
"Hullo, Trudl! Woud you like to come down
and help me with these?"*

*I waived back. "Not just now, thanks, Mrs.
Sanderson."*

"All right, dear. Later, if you like."

*So now I couldn't chuck it out. She woud
have seen me. She woud have been schocked
and woud have sayd, "How coud you chuck
out your preshus heirloom emerald?"*

*I shut the window then. I turned to the
dolls. They sat together on top of the chest of
drawers. And suddenly the story about*

66

Felicity-Emma got realler than real, and now Nirob wanted to be in it also.

"Don't, don't chuck out the emerald," Felicity-Emma seemed to call to me clearer than clearly, "I want to stay alive!"

Nirob wanted to, also. But his lips are painted shut.

I took them both down from the chest of drawers. I sat down on my bed with them. I took them on my lap. And I wrote with the emerald between my thumb and forfinger, in invisibel writing, on both their bodies over where their hearts would be:

"Be alive forever."

I knew now what I'd do. It was easy. But my hand, my hole self, shook. It was the most seecret thing I ever have done. I will never tell it to anybody in the world as long as I live. And I whispered to the emerald, under my breath:

From this day on, in darkness shine!
Do no more harm. But still be mine!

Just then a jangling pierced the air—the doorbell! Apricot Jones leaped off the bed. Jenny's heart turned over.

The bell rang again, insistently.

"I'm coming!" Jenny called with shaking voice. Her knees shook as she climbed on the desk and quickly put the copybook back.

Then she went and opened the door—"Mom!"

"Jenny, are you okay? I was so worried! I let the phone ring and ring! Why didn't you answer it?"

"Um—" Jenny started, with no idea where that would lead.

"Were you on the toilet?"

"Yes. Yes, I was!"

"Are you sure you're okay?" Mom peered at her. It was dark in the hall. Mom switched the overhead light on. "You look kind of pale."

"I'm okay," said Jenny. In her whole life, she had hardly ever lied to Mom. Now, in less than a minute, she had lied twice in a row: about being on the toilet. And about being okay. That was the bigger lie. Anyone who did what she had been doing was definitely not okay.

"Daddy's on his way home," Mom said. "So I thought we'd have an early dinner. Are you just about through here?"

"Just about," Jenny echoed vaguely. "Except I haven't fed the cats yet."

"Well, do it."

Jenny fed them. Then she filled up the watering can.

"You mean to say, you didn't water the plants yet either?"

"Not all."

"What *did* you do?"

"I watered some. I fed Augusta."

"You've been up here for over an hour!" Mom tipped Jenny's chin up and looked her in the eyes.

"What have you been doing all this time?"

Jenny longed to get it off her chest. "Well, you see, Mom," she began, "I found this old cop—" No, she couldn't. She couldn't tell anyone, not even Mom. That would make it an even worse betrayal.

"This old what?" Mom asked.

"This old copy—copy of *Black Beauty*," Jenny lied, for the third time.

"*Black Beauty?* I thought you already read that."

"I did. I started to read it again." Jenny lowered her eyes. She wondered if "I bloody well curse you forever" had already started to work its harm by turning her into such a big liar.

She ate very little and was quiet at dinner. Her parents thought this was because of night-before excitement about the trip.

Later, Mom came into her room to help her pack. They packed everything except April and Esther. "Are you taking them both?" Mom asked. "Should we pack them, or will you carry them?"

"I'm not taking them."

"Oh? Why not?"

"I don't know. I just don't think I should."

"I don't see why not," said Mom. "At least one of them. Sleep on it, Jenny. Maybe you'll change your mind."

Lying in bed, Jenny thought, I'm not trying to prove how grown-up I am, or anything like that. I know I'll miss them. But I won't change my mind.

Oddly, that decision made her feel better.

And she did not have nightmares. In fact, she had a good dream in which she told Aunt Trudl everything, and Aunt Trudl laughed and said, "Don't worry, it's okay."

Next morning—*the* day!—she woke up at seven thirty feeling terrific, and starved for breakfast. She put on her new outfit for traveling: dark blue knit pants, a drip-dry light blue beautiful shirt, and a blue-and-red sweater she looked really good in.

She waited around till she heard her parents' alarm go off. Then she called, "I'm going to Aunt Trudl's!"

She took the stairs rather than wait for the elevator. And she rehearsed how she would tell Aunt Trudl, "Well, you see, it was really an accident. If Murrna hadn't knocked it down, I never would have found it. But there it was. So I started to read it. I stopped at the page with the warning, and that curse—remember? But then yesterday, when I was up here again, I couldn't help it, I tried not to, honest,"—now the words would rush out, fast—"I was just so curious about what was going to happen, I had to go on reading, so I did, to where you did that most secret thing. Only then Mom came, so I had to stop. Oh, Aunt Trudl, I hope you're not angry, I hope you don't mind too much!" And she could practically already see her smile, and hear her say, "No, I don't mind. It's okay, don't worry about it."

Then, Jenny imagined, Aunt Trudl would ask, "Where is that old copybook, anyway? I haven't seen it in ages." And Jenny would get it down, and she and Aunt Trudl would read it together.

She stood in front of Aunt Trudl's apartment. She never used her own keys when Aunt Trudl was home. She rang the bell.

Seven

But it was Silverman, not Aunt Trudl, who opened the door. He was a tall, elegantly slim old man with silvergray hair, silver-rimmed glasses, and a luxuriant long moustache. Just now he wore a dishtowel tucked into his belt and held a wire whisk in his hand.

Jenny blurted out, "What are *you* doing here?"

Not that he wasn't often around, not that she didn't like him. She liked him okay. In fact, she used to wonder why he and Aunt Trudl didn't get married. She had asked Aunt Trudl about that. "Why should we?" Aunt Trudl asked back. "We're fine the way we are. We like to be alone, too, sometimes, and we like having our own apartments." She'd kidded Jenny, "You just want to be a bridesmaid at a wedding." And they had sung, "Here comes the bride,/ All fat and wide" (which Aunt Trudl was not, though she was not exactly skinny and narrow, either). Jenny had grabbed the tablecloth off the table and put it over Aunt

Trudl's head, and they'd marched through the living room, Jenny carrying Aunt Trudl's train.

It was just that Jenny wasn't glad to see Silverman now, when she needed so badly to talk to Aunt Trudl alone.

"Good morning, World Traveler," Silverman said pleasantly. "It so happens, I'm making *Palatschinken.*" Those really were a Viennese dessert: dainty pancakes filled with jam, sprinkled with powdered sugar, not at all easy to prepare. "Trudl said that's what we're having for your farewell breakfast. She's still asleep, so I thought I'd start."

"That's really nice of you." Jenny felt like two cents for being rude before.

They went into the kitchen.

The table was already set. Silverman said, whisking the *Palatschinken* batter, "Feed the cats, would you, Jenny?"

Murrna and Apricot Jones were pacing back and forth in front of the refrigerator.

Jenny poured them some milk. Then she opened the dark corner cabinet where the cat food was kept—and took a scared jump backward. "Hey! There's something in there!" She threw the door shut.

"What?"

"I don't know! It looked like green fire!"

Silverman laughed. "It's only Mephisto. Since when are you scared of him?"

The cabinet door swung open, and, sure enough, Mephisto walked out, blinking innocently at the light, waving his orange-tipped tail and meowing for his breakfast.

"You devil!" Jenny was mad at him. She shoved him with her foot as he tried to shoulder his way past Murrna and Apricot Jones to the milk.

She put out cat food. "It's almost ten after eight. Aunt Trudl said I should come at eight. I'm going to wake her."

"Give her five more minutes," Silverman said. "We got back very late last night."

At eight thirteen, Jenny went into the bedroom-study and woke her.

She rubbed her eyes. "Hi, Jenny. That travel outfit looks terrific on you! Did I oversleep?"

Jenny nodded.

Aunt Trudl put on her old plaid bathrobe that looked like a horse blanket. "Is my nose deceiving me? How can it be that I smell *Palatschinken?*"

"Silverman's making some. Aunt Trudl, listen, I have to tell you someth—"

"Wait till I brush my teeth." She went into the bathroom.

After the bathroom Aunt Trudl went in the kitchen and put her arms around Silverman's dishtowel-covered waist. "Silverman, you are a truly liberated man." She kissed him on the back of the shoulder.

He put a gob of butter in a pan. It sizzled. He poured some batter in. "Sit down, Trudl. You too, Jenny. Drink your juice."

Soon he served them each a *Palatschinke.*

74

A CERTAIN MAGIC

"That's the best I've ever tasted," said Aunt Trudl, eating hers.

Jenny only took one bite.

"Isn't it light enough?" Silverman asked worriedly.

"It's fine. I'm just not hungry."

"For your farewell breakfast? That's a shame. Maybe the scare Mephisto gave you took away your appetite."

"Mephisto scared Jenny?" Aunt Trudl laughed. "How did he manage that?"

"He was hiding in that cabinet, and all I could see was his eyes. They looked like a devil's eyes." Jenny emphasized the word *devil*. She hoped it would make Aunt Trudl think of the copybook, so it would be easier to tell her about it.

"You've been watching horror movies," Aunt Trudl said.

"I think she has a slight case of jet jitters," Silverman said. "I always do, till I get on the plane. Then, you'll see, you'll feel fine, you'll love being in the air, and you'll love all the food, it always tastes extra good."

"I haven't watched horror movies. I don't have jet jitters. I just have to tell you something."

Silverman took the hint that it needed to be said in private, and retired to the bathroom with *The New York Times*.

Aunt Trudl helped herself to another *Palatschinke*. "Okay, I'm listening."

75

But now that they were alone, the words Jenny had rehearsed wouldn't come.

Aunt Trudl finished eating. "That was some festive breakfast you didn't have. Oh, well. Come talk to me while I get dressed."

They went into the bedroom-study. Jenny sat down—on the very bed on which she had lain, reading Aunt Trudl's secrets. . . .

"Now tell me what's on your mind," said Aunt Trudl in such a loving voice, Jenny felt a hundred times guiltier.

Tears came into her eyes. "I'm a crybaby too, just like you were." She hoped that word, "crybaby," would remind her.

Aunt Trudl put on a sweater and skirt. "Hey, hey," she said, seeing the tears on Jenny's face, and sat down next to her. "What is it? Come on!"

Jenny tried to see past Aunt Trudl's wrinkles, to think them away, think the gray in her hair away, and what she was wearing away. She squeezed her eyes shut for a second and with all her might tried to conjure back the girl, eleven and a half, in the white summer dress with poppies on it.

She couldn't.

But at least Aunt Trudl's eyes didn't look old. They looked as if they could still see back that far, as if they could still remember . . .

Remember the copybook! Guess that I found it and read it! Say it's all right! Jenny begged her silently, via ESP.

"It's ten of nine," Silverman called. "I'm going

over to the garage for the station wagon. I'll meet you downstairs in ten minutes, okay?"

"Okay," Aunt Trudl called back, putting her left shoe on. The right one was under the bed. She crouched down to get it. "Jenny, if you're going to tell me, you'd better do it fast."

"Well, you see, Aunt Trudl, I—I can't! Do you believe in magic?"

"Of course not." Both shoes on now, Aunt Trudl went to the bureau. While pinning back her hair, she caught sight of the picture next to the mirror, of the orange and blue flowers in the crystal vase. She loved that picture. "I take back what I said. I guess I do believe in a certain kind of magic—"

"That's not what I mean!" Panic crept into Jenny's voice as time was running out. "I mean magic, like that there's a devil, and there could be magic curses, stuff like that."

"That doesn't sound like you! What have you been reading? *Weirda Witch Comics?*"

The phone rang. It was Mom, Jenny knew.

"Okay, she'll be right down. Silverman went for the station wagon. Meet you downstairs in five minutes."

"She wants me to check that I didn't forget anything, doesn't she?" Jenny said.

"That's right."

Jenny scooped up Apricot Jones, who'd been playing with Aunt Trudl's slipper, in her arms. "I don't even have time to say good-bye to the others. Apricot, tell them good-bye for me. Augusta,

77

too." Jenny buried her face in the cat's furry side and said in a muffled voice, "Oh, Apricot, why can't you talk? Then you could tell what I did, and I wouldn't have to."

Aunt Trudl heard. "You don't have to. Whoever said that people have to tell each other everything they do?"

On the ride to Kennedy Airport, Aunt Trudl sat in front with Silverman. Jenny sat in back between her parents.

Mom worried about things she might have forgotten: "Did I call off the *Times* delivery service? Did I turn the burner off under the coffee pot? Did I double-lock the door?"

"Yes, yes, you did," Daddy assured her.

"But I really forgot something!" The thought hit Jenny with a pang: She hadn't called Nancy. And she'd promised. And she couldn't do it from the airport because today was a school day. She must feel really hurt! She must be really mad at me, Jenny thought, and in her mind she saw the copybook page with the warning on it, and the picture of the ring and all the little lines reaching out from the emerald, as though they were reaching into the future, into now, on to whoever had read on and was cursed. . . .

She thought of her dolls, April and Esther, sitting deserted on her bed in the darkened apartment. Now she knew why she had decided not to bring them: as a sacrifice, a kind of bribe to the curse, to make it leave her alone. But that hadn't worked. And the curse *was* working, she could tell, or she wouldn't have broken her promise to Nancy.

Inside the airline terminal, after they'd already said good-bye, Aunt Trudl said, "Jenny, it's too great a day to look like thunder-weather." With her two index fingers she pulled the corners of Jenny's mouth up into a smile. "I bet whatever's bothering you isn't as bad as you think."

"It is. You just don't know."

"Well, I can think of something worse."

"Like what?"

"If you let it keep you from having a fabulous trip. That would be worse. Promise you won't let it do that."

Jenny could not promise. But she said, "I'll try."

The engines revving up made a tremendous roar. The jet was huge, as much bigger than a person as a tree is bigger than a bug. Yet Jenny felt the roaring as if it were happening inside her. She readied herself, just like the airplane readied itself, for the tremendous moment . . . she held her breath . . . she gripped the armrests hard . . . NOW!

"Daddy, now! Look!" She let go of one armrest and gripped his hand.

He leaned over to see out her window.

The landing gear had left the ground. The jet soared up. How slowly it seemed to climb! Yet in a second they were high up in the blue air.

The runway below turned into a ribbon. "I feel like a giant," Jenny said, surprised that her voice still sounded as it always did, instead of giant loud. "I feel as if I'm flying!"

"Well, you are," said Daddy.

"I don't mean just in a plane, I mean, myself! I've never felt like this, it's so great! Do you feel that way, Daddy? Do you, Mom?"

They both smiled. Mom said, "Not exactly."

Daddy said, "It's a big improvement over how you felt just a short while ago, isn't it? What was wrong with you? I couldn't help overhearing Aunt Trudl tell you not to let something or other spoil the trip. What was that all about?"

Out the window, down below, Long Island looked like a map. Cars and trucks on the roads, houses, whole towns had dwindled to toy size. Jenny thought, If I was down there, I'd be a thousand times smaller than an ant. And my whole trouble would be—oh, about a million times smaller than an ant's egg.

"It was nothing," she answered her father. "Anyway, I don't want to talk about it. Look, there's Jones Beach! Or is it Far Rockaway? And look, there goes a boat on the ocean, it's the size of a peanut shell! This is so terrific, I never thought anything could be like this! I want to fly all the time, I think I'll be a pilot—um, tomato juice, please."

The airplane hostess had come and was asking what everyone wanted to drink.

A CERTAIN MAGIC

Mom and Daddy ordered champagne. Jenny
took a sip from Mom's, then from Daddy's plastic
glass. "Easy," said Daddy. "You're pretty high as
it is."

"Sure I am!" Jenny hiccupped. "How can anyone not be, up here?"

Lunch was beef stew with a long French name.
Mom and Daddy joked about how the knives,
forks, salt, pepper, salad dressing, everything,
came individually wrapped in plastic. "It tastes
plastic, too," said Mom, taking a bite.

"It does not," said Jenny.

"I thought you can't stand beef stew," said
Daddy.

"I can't, down on the ground. Up here, it's delicious. Silverman was right, everything tastes extra
good if you eat it while you're flying."

After lunch came the movie. Jenny was amazed
how many people watched it, instead of looking
out their windows. She'd seen lots of movies in her
life. But never before now had she seen the top
sides of clouds, clouds below, instead of overhead!
They kept changing shapes and colors. First they
looked like somebody had transported every
woolly white sheep from the whole earth to up
here. Then they looked more like herds of buffalo,
and some like elephants, and some like mountains.
Then they separated into two cloud-continents
with a wide stretch of blue ocean—no, air—in between.

Jenny felt like trying to draw some of this. But

it was dark inside the plane on account of the movie. And the airline hostesses weren't bringing stuff like pencils and paper to people while the movie was going on. Besides, she thought, why spoil my mood? I'd just get disappointed because whatever I could draw would turn out so much less fantastic than what I'm really looking at.

She kept on looking out the window as the plane flew east, leaving the sun farther and farther behind. The people across the aisle could have been watching the sun go down out their windows if they hadn't been watching the movie. The clouds on Jenny's side turned from white to rosy, to glowing, to purplish, then to gray and grayer as the plane speeded above them into cloudless dark blueness rapidly darkening to black.

When the movie was over and the lights came on, she looked at her watch—twenty past three! She asked, "Is that the right time, Daddy?"

Her father checked his watch. "Yes, but that's New York time. In London it's twenty after nine." He set his watch ahead.

Jenny set hers ahead too, and she thought, Six hours wiped out of existence, just like chalk marks off a blackboard! Just as though they'd never been! She knew, of course, that European time was different from American. They had studied that in science last year, in fifth grade. And she had been watching it happen out the window, daylight turning so fast into night. Still, the idea flabbergasted her. Six hours erased just like that, with just a few twists of the watch winder! And whoever said—this thought came to her like a brainstorm—that all six hours had to come out of today?

"Whhhhsh!" With a flick of the wrist she erased one hour and a half, from four to five thirty, out of yesterday afternoon. So much for that hour and a half alone up at Aunt Trudl's! It was wiped out, gone, nothing! And she had nothing to blame herself for, nothing on her conscience!

"What are you grinning about?" Daddy asked.

"Nothing!" she said thinking. Nothing, is right! So now nothing can't spoil the trip for me, can it? She could just imagine the look on Miss Dreyfuss, her English teacher's face at such grammar, and hear her say teasingly, "Nothing can't?" She thought, That's right, Miss Dreyfuss, nothing can't. Nothing won't, either. Or was it neither? Wondering about that, she started to giggle and did not stop till her father popped a peppermint Lifesaver into her mouth.

Eight

CARRON'S HOTEL
LONDON, W.1

Sunday night

Dear Nancy,

I hope you aren't still mad at me that I didn't call you. I'm really sorry I didn't. I would have written sooner. But I didn't have time. We have been sightseeing our feet off! Well, maybe not our feet, but yesterday Mom's heel came off her shoe, from all the walking. And I have a hole in my sole—hey, that rhymes! If I wrote you all the sights we already saw, this letter would get as long as a book.

So far what I like best are: double-decker buses, Indian food, Big Ben, and parks. Yesterday, right at noon, we stood right under Big Ben. I closed my ears for half the BONGs. They were still plenty loud. In Re-

gent's Park we rowed on a lake. In Hyde Park we heard a band concert. They played that thing from Gilbert and Sullivan, "Hey Dee Hey Dee, Misery Me," that you like so much. I wished you could have heard it.

At night all the buildings along the Thames and some bridges are lit up really bright like at a fair.

But guess what: London Bridge is in Arizona! They moved it there, I don't know why.

We have not been in any museums—yet. But we have seen some from outside, and they look HUGE. Tomorrow Daddy has to do some work. So I'll just be with Mom. And something tells me, Museums, here we come.

Did you have a nice time at S. Susan Morris's house? Did she brag to you about who all she's "going steady" with?

I hope you're having a good vacation. And that when I get home I'll still be

Your best friend,
Jenny

P.S. I think there's a canary in this hotel! At least I thought I heard one sing, when we first arrived. But that was at two thirty A.M., and maybe I had jet lag and was hearing things. I'll let you know. Love, J

That same evening she also wrote two picture postcards to Aunt Trudl.

One was of a red double-decker bus.

Dear Aunt Trudl,

I said BAGS (to myself, not out loud). X marks where I sat, on top, by the window. London's great! I love buses, curries, saffron, the lakes in the parks, Big Ben, and grilled to-mahtoes. But I haven't seen any sidewalk pictures yet. Mom and Daddy think there may not be any more sidewalk artists. I hope there are.

Love, Jenny

The other card was of the long lagoon with ducks and swans in St. James's Park.

Dear Aunt Trudl,

X marks the spot where I threw in some bread for ducklings. XX marks the spot whre I saw pelicans, just like you said! I tried a kipper for breakfast today. Palatschinken are better. Say hello to Silverman.

Love, Jenny

At breakfast Monday, Jenny and Mom's day together, Mom suggested, "Let's not go to too many places today. Let's just go to one place you really want to, and one place I really want to. Okay?"

That evening Jenny wrote on a picture postcard of a mother koala bear with her cubs:

Dear Nancy,

We went to a small museum. It had only three rooms! It wasn't too bad. Then we went to Regent's Park Zoo. That was great! I hope the stuffed koala bears on your bed like the real ones on this card.

Love, Jenny

After that, Jenny wrote to Aunt Trudl. She had bought a postcard for her at the small museum of a painting of a cozy, cluttered room with plants on the window and the sun shining in and a cat walking around a bumpy-looking couch with different-colored cushions on it.

Dear Aunt Trudl,

Guess what this painting reminds me of! Today Mom and I went to the museum where this painting is. And guess where else: to Regent's Park Zoo. Mom rode on a camel there. The only kind of animal we did not see was a monkey on a string doing acro—

Damn it, what did I write that for? Jenny crossed the last sentence out with such heavy pen strokes, they showed through to the picture side. The card looked a mess.

I can't send it like that, she thought, starting to feel as she had not felt since the airplane: bothered again. Guilty. That hour and a half was sneaking back—of course it was. You couldn't really erase any hours out of time, even if you spent your whole life up in airplanes. Deep down, she had really known this all along.

Nine

The feeling of having to go to the bathroom woke her out of deep sleep the next night. She did not realize that she was not at home in her own bed. She staggered up and walked to the left, across the room, as she would have done at home. Only here the bathroom was to the right. She went through a door—not the bathroom door. And the door fell shut.

Now she realized where she was. I'm locked out! What'll I do?

She crossed the dim, night-quiet hotel corridor and knocked at her parents' door. They had gone to the theater and to supper afterward. They were still out.

Well, there was a W.C. downstairs, way at the far end of the lobby. I'll have to walk that whole long way, just in shorty pajamas, some fun, she thought. But what else could she do?

She pressed the button for the elevator but changed her mind. She couldn't wait that long. She took the stairs instead.

The lobby was as long as a whole city block. It went from the front entrance to the hotel on one street to the rear entrance on the next street. It was furnished with groups of chairs, couches, tables, and lamps. Now all but one of the lamps were turned off. It was very dark. Jenny hoped she wouldn't bang into anything. She hoped even more that a whole bunch of people would not pick now of all times to come in and see her rushing by.

No one came in. Only the night clerk saw her. His name was Mr. Fitzsimmons—she remembered seeing the nameplate on his desk the night they arrived. He was tall and bald, with a paunch of a belly. He wore the same dark brown coat as the other night. It had brass buttons, and tails in the back like a giant beetle's. "Can I 'elp you, Miss?" he called to her.

"No, it's okay, I'm just going to—" She didn't have to name it, she was was already there. Happiness is getting to the john, I mean, W.C., in time, she thought, closing the door, sitting down.

It was an old-fashioned toilet, the kind with a water tank up on the wall, and a pull chain for flushing. She pulled. Water roared down, as loud as Niagara Falls.

Happiness will now be followed by having to ask that Mr. Fitzsimmons guy to let me back in my room. Oh, well, thought Jenny, if anybody ever asks me what was the most embarrassing moment of my life, I'll know what to say. And she started the long way back.

Halfway through the lobby, she heard a chirp. Then she heard a burble. Then she saw a small wire cage standing on Mr. Fitzsimmons's desk. I knew it, I knew it, she thought, forgetting her embarrassment and coming nearer, on tiptoes, so as not to scare the canary.

The chirp and burble had been merely a warm-up. Now the canary was singing. Out of his beak came the most beautiful sounds—more beautiful than when Nancy sang, and she had the best voice in school; more beautiful than when Beverly Sills or Judy Collins sang. She hoped the canary would sing on and on.

But soon he stopped. And all her embarrassment returned. "Um, er, you see, I—" she started to explain why she had had to come down here.

"Of course," Mr. Fitzsimmons interrupted with the most understanding smile. "Believe me, I could own this 'otel and a few more besides, if I 'ad a shilling for every guest that's ever been in your shoes." He glanced down, saw that she was barefoot, and he laughed, such a friendly laugh, so full of pleasure at having someone to talk to, that Jenny laughed too.

"You're the young American lady, Miss Ehrenteil, aren't you?" Only he pronounced it "Hurnthile."

She nodded. "My first name's Jenny."

"Ah, Jenny—a lovely name," said Mr. Fitzsimmons. "And this 'ere is Nelson." He offered her some birdseed to feed to the canary.

"He's a terrific singer," said Jenny.

"That 'e is. And I'll tell you something about Nelson: 'E's particular. 'E only sings for people 'e likes."

"I'm glad," said Jenny. Mr. Fitzsimmons had put her so much at ease she thought, I'm almost glad I locked myself out, or I wouldn't have found out about Nelson. And she asked, "How come I didn't see him when we first got here?"

"I put his cage down back there." Mr. Fitzsimmons pointed to the corner behind the desk. "It wouldn't be proper for Nelson to be chirping away when I'm busy receiving 'otel guests."

"Did you name him after the Admiral Nelson whose statue is on top of that big tall column in Trafalgar Square?"

"No. After Nelson Eddy. 'E was a film star, and a fine singer, too. But a bit before your time."

They went on chatting for a while, about the sights of London, and about the weather. "It's a shame, all the rain we're 'avin'," Mr. Fitzsimmons apologized, as though he personally were responsible for it.

"It rains just as much in New York in April," Jenny said to make him feel better.

Then Nelson gave an encore.

Then Mr. Fitzsimmons took out a bunch of keys and let Jenny back into her room. And when he wished her a good night he called her Miss Hurn-thile again.

He probably never calls any hotel guests by their first names, not even kids, Jenny figured. "Good night, Mr. Fitzsimmons. Thanks a lot."

"Not at all. Be sure you come and see us again before you go back to America." He sounded as though he really wanted her to.

So she said, "I will."

She wrote right away, on a postcard of the hotel:

> Dear Nancy,
>   There is a canary here! The way I found out was, I locked myself out of my room by mistake, and had to go down to the lobby, in just my pajamas, to the W.C. Guess what that is. I was so embarrassed I thought I'd die. Instead I heard Nelson, that's the canary's name. I wish you and he could sing a duet. It's the middle of the night now, but I said I'd let you know. (Even though I'll probably see you before this card gets there!)
>   Love, Jenny

Ten

Wednesday night, our stay is two thirds over,
Jenny wrote at the top of a sheet of hotel station-
ery. But this was not going to be a letter to anyone. She only wrote this for herself, to see if putting it on paper could make it less awful in her
mind.

Today I saw Adolf Hitler.

It wouldn't have happened if we'd gone to the
British Museum with Mom. But Mom said Daddy
and I could go some place else if we wanted to,
that would be all right with her. So we went to
Madame Tussaud's. That is one place I'll never go
near again as long as I live.

First there was a huge room, the Grand Hall. It
had about a hundred wax figures of kings, queens,
presidents, and popes from long ago to now. Some
were standing up. Some were sitting down. Some
looked into nowhere. Some gave others dirty
looks. We were surprised how short they all
seemed, even Abraham Lincoln. And their faces
were kind of yellow and dead looking. Except for

the ones who were supposed to be black, like Emperor Haile Selassie and President Jomo Kenyatta. Their faces were muddy-gray-brownish, and dead looking too. You could tell right away, even if you didn't know what this place was all about, that they were made of wax.

Then there was another room, not so big, with not so many lights. In there they had figures of Twiggy and rock stars—Mick Jagger, people like that. Some of those looked a little more real, maybe because they weren't so bunched together.

Next was supposed to be the Chamber of Horrors. It had poisoners and stranglers and people who got hanged or had their heads chopped off, Daddy said. He asked if I was sure I wanted to go in there. He was kidding. He knows that wouldn't frighten me.

I said, "Sure." He went straight in. I took a couple of steps, then stopped. I felt like I'd been turned to wax myself. I felt like I couldn't move. Because just before the Chamber of Horrors door, there stood Hitler. Not with a bunch of Nazis, or anybody. By himself. He had one leg out, as if he was coming straight at me. He stared me in the face. And he didn't look made of wax one bit.

I always thought that Hitler had piercing brown eyes, like Dr. Kessel's, the pediatrician I went to when I was little, whom I hated. Well, this Hitler had blue eyes. They didn't look exactly friendly. But they did not look piercing, either, or especially horrible. They looked ordinary, just like *anybody's eyes. I don't know why, but that almost scared me the most.*

This sounds crazy, but I thought, maybe he isn't really dead. I felt as if he knew me. As if he might call me "Fräulein Ehrenteil" and say, "Do you see my moustache? It has still all its moustache hairs, jawohl! (That means "yes, indeed" in German.)

I was so scared, I felt as if the whole place was spinning around. "Daddy!" I yelled. Thank God he was just coming back looking for me. I was never so glad to see anybody in my whole life. He put his arm around me, "Let's skip the Chamber of Horrors," he said. We got out of Madame Tussaud's fast.

It was raining when we came, but now it was sunny out. Daddy said, "We're right near Regent's Park." So we went there for a while, and sat down on a bench. He wanted me to tell him why I got so panicky. He didn't think Hitler having blue eyes was a good enough reason.

While we were sitting there, a bunch of girls around my age came down the path. They all had green blazers on over green and white dresses. I guess they were on a field trip with their class or something like that. Anyway, they were horsing around, teasing each other, and talking loud, but with such British accents, I couldn't understand what they said. Two of them looked over at us. Then they whispered to each other and laughed. Maybe they weren't even laughing at me. But I suddenly felt stupid in my jeans and raincoat. Like a

*sore thumb. Like a foreigner. Like Aunt Trudl
must have felt.*

*I couldn't explain it any better to Daddy about
what happened to me with that Hitler. I can't explain it any better to myself. All I know is, if I
hadn't read the copybook, that Hitler at Madame
Tussaud's wouldn't have bothered me one bit.*

*Only three and a half more days, and we'll be
on the plane. Even though I loved it so much,
being in the air, I can't look forward to it now. I
just keep thinking about how we'll turn our
watches back, and put all those hours back into
time.*

*It's late. I'm really tired. I wish I had Esther or
April. It was stupid of me not to bring at least one
of them. I wish Apricot Jones was here.*

Jenny drew a picture of her. But it didn't look
like Apricot Jones one bit. She crossed it out with
a lot of thick pen lines and went on writing.

*I wish I'd never ~~layed~~ laid eyes on that copy-
book. Or that I could have finished reading to the
end. I wish, I wish I knew if that emerald is still
anywhere, shining in darkness, like it said in that
rhyme. What darkness? And did it ever really
have magic? Does it still? Or is that all a bunch of
Blodsin. (I don't remember how to spell that word—*

"Oh, what the hell, it didn't help a bit to write
all this." She tore it up and went to bed.

Eleven

On Thursday, walking down a street near the Chelsea Embankment, Jenny saw the sidewalk picture. It was of a garden. There were other pictures too: of a castle, of a bridge, of rooftops, of mountains. But Jenny scarcely glanced at those. She could not take her eyes off the garden one. She felt as if she recognized it. She thought, I *know* that place.

Daddy said, "Well, I'm glad there still are sidewalk artists." He and Mom looked at the pictures for about a second and walked on.

"Hey, come back! Look at this," Jenny called. "Isn't it beautiful?"

They came back, but they were impatient. "It's too pretty," said Mom in her art-teacher voice.

"You've looked at it long enough. Let's go," said Daddy, and he listed a lot of places in this section of London that he wanted to see.

Jenny did not want to move from this spot.

She had read a book once about a boy who liked a picture so much, he had found a way to get inside it, and had lived in the picture for a while instead of where he really lived. She thought, I wish I could do that.

In the middle of the garden was a lush green lawn. You could tell by the dapples of sunlight and dark shady patches that the time was early morning. You could almost fell the dew. To the right of the lawn were rose bushes covered with roses in all possible, and some impossible, rose colors: white, yellow, orange, candy pink, salmon pink, bright red, and deep, dark purple, almost black. To the left of the lawn there were other flowers, every imaginable kind, in all imaginable colors, in all sizes, from tiny, close to the ground, to tall and spiky. At the far side were flowering bushes. Behind those a pebbled path led out of the picture. And out of the distance, down that path, came a slender, rust-colored, wavy-haired dog, an Irish setter—Ballou! Jenny thought. And these—some low-growing orange flowers with round leaves—these could be Mark's nasturtiums, this could be his garden bed, where they buried the goldfish. And there Trudl pricked her finger picking a rose. And over by those petunias, that's where Mrs. Sanderson would have been gardening, when Trudl nearly chucked the emerald out the window into that grass. . . .

"I have to go there!" said Jenny out loud.

"Go where?" her parents asked.

"To Twiford. Listen, Mom, listen, Daddy, it isn't too far. And I want to go there so much!"

"*What* is it?" Mom asked.

"The place where Aunt Trudl stayed. You know about it, don't you, Daddy?"

"You mean when she was a little girl, before the war? All I know is, she stayed with a family near London somewhere."

"Well, it was in Twiford. And we should go there."

"Why?"

"What for?"

"I can't explain it to you. I just know we should."

Her parents looked bewildered. Daddy said, "If Trudl had wanted us to, she'd have said something. Did she, to you?"

Mom asked, "Did she tell you about the place, and what it's like there?"

"No," Jenny admitted. "I just want to go there."

"But why?" both her parents asked.

"Because this picture is making me want to!"

They shook their heads. Daddy said, "That doesn't make sense."

"Mom, don't *you* know what I mean? Didn't a picture ever make you want to go to some place really badly?"

"Oh, sure. I've seen some wonderful paintings of Venice. And some of the hills around Florence And there's one I love most, of the Garden of Eden. They all made me feel that way. But I still haven't been to any of those places. And anyway, what does this picture have to do with Twiford?"

100

"I don't know. I just have a feeling—"

"Well, I have a feeling I'd rather stay in London than traipse to some place we know nothing about," said Mom. And Daddy agreed with her.

Just then, out of the Golden Lion, a pub across the street, came a sandy-haired man in a baggy suit toward them. He had a short cigarette butt sticking out of his mouth as if it were permanently attached there. He held his cap out with pride, yet also with shame at asking for money.

"I think that's the artist," said Jenny.

Mom and Daddy dropped twenty pence in his cap.

"Much obliged," he muttered with a shrug that said louder than words, My work is worth a damned sight more.

Jenny had a pound note in her coat pocket. She smoothed it out and handed it to him.

"I thank you kindly, Miss." He smiled at her without dislodging the butt. The smile meant, That's a bit more like it. And he crossed the street, back toward the pub.

"Jenny!" said Mom. "Have you any idea how much money you just gave away?"

"Sure. Two dollars and forty cents. That picture's worth it."

"Uh uh. It's corny. The perspective's all wrong."

"It is *not* corny. Who cares about the perspective?"

"Don't speak to Mom in that tone," said Daddy.

101

"You'll care tomorrow when we go to Bermondsey and you don't have enough money left to buy
presents," said Mom.

"I don't want to go to Bermondsey!"

"After all your pestering about going to a street
market? I don't know what's gotten into you,
Jenny. You're acting like a brat. Come on, Harry."
The two of them walked abruptly away.

Jenny stood there as long as she dared, letting
the sidewalk picture of the garden engrave itself
into her mind. Then she went after them.

For the rest of the day they took turns telling
Jenny things like: Now's your chance to see this
house where famous old Whozits lived. Now is the
only time in your life you may ever be standing in
this historic old church. Or in this historic old
graveyard where the historic old bones of well-
known old What's-his-name lie. So appreciate it.

Jenny couldn't.

"You weren't exactly good company today,"
Daddy told her at dinner.

Mom put it still more bluntly: "You were lousy
company. You sulked, you grouched, and I bet
your fingernails are sore from all the biting." She
was right. They were.

After dinner Jenny went to her room, took her
sketch pad and pastels, and tried to draw the garden. It was impossibly hard. Her first four tries
ended in the wastebasket.

She was on her fifth try when Mom came in.
Mom and Daddy were invited to a party at the

house of some people Daddy had met on business. Mom wore a cream-colored dress that showed off her figure.

"You look nice, Mom," said Jenny, tearing the fifth try off the sketch pad. She was about to crumple it up and throw it in the wastebasket too, when Mom said, "Let me see," and took it from her.

"Mm." She studied it. "That's pretty good, Jenny."

"It isn't! I couldn't get anywhere near as many flowers in as there were on the sidewalk picture. And I don't have enough colors."

"It looks like plenty of flowers to me. And I really like that tree stump at the edge of the lawn, it makes the whole scene more realistic—"

"I didn't even mean to put a tree stump there! I tried to draw Bal—I mean, a rust-brown dog. I don't have a rust-brown pastel, though, so I tried mixing colors. But they came out all wrong. And anyway, I couldn't draw a dog from memory, it came out like a blob. The only thing I could do was turn it into this dumb old stump."

"It's not dumb." Mom smiled. "You'd be surprised, sometimes the best parts of pictures come about just like that. Can I have it when it's finished?"

Jenny shook her head. She thought Mom was just being extra nice to make up for before. "It's okay, Mom. It's true what you said, I *was* lousy company. I couldn't help it. I'm sorry."

103

"I was pretty rough on you," Mom said. She played with a strand of Jenny's hair, winding and unwinding it around her finger. "I wish you could let me in on the secret of that sidewalk garden."

Jenny put her face against Mom's shoulder. "I wish I could too. But I can't, Mom."

Mom looked sad. She studied the picture some more. "Is it okay if I use these, Jenny?"

"Sure, go ahead."

Mom picked up two of the pastels, the red one and the white one. "Now watch." She made a patch of red on a piece of sketching paper. Then she put a bit of white over it and blended it to pink by rubbing it with the tip of her little finger.

"That's exactly the color pink I wanted for the petunias!"

"You can blend pastels together and get just about any tint or shade of any color. It takes a little practice, that's all." Mom put the pastels back in their box. "Don't do too much more tonight, Jen. Go to bed pretty soon. We want to be at Bermondsey before nine tomorrow." She kissed her good night, started for the door, turned around, and said, "Tomorrow morning, get out on the right side of bed, all right?"

"D'you believe in that, Mom?"

Mom shook her head. "You know I don't. It's just a way of asking you to make tomorrow a good day. Good night now, Jenny."

"Good night, Mom. Have fun at the party."

104

A CERTAIN MAGIC

As soon as Mom left, Jenny took the green pastel and started another picture: of the emerald. She made it big, so it would be easier to work on. First she made it all green. Then she put white and yellow highlights in, to show its many surfaces and how they glistened. Then she blended in some blue toward the bottom, to show how deep it was. She used the tip of her finger the way Mom had done. Next, she drew lots of little lines, like there were around the copybook picture of the ring. She alternated green, yellow, orange, pink, red, blue, even purple, to show the emerald's radiance.

When she finished, it really was radiant. It really looked like an emerald.

She held it at arm's length. It's beautiful, she thought. It even looks mysterious, as if it could be magical. I've never done such a good picture before. And she wondered if in some mysterious way the real emerald's magic could have been reaching her while she was drawing. Could that explain why this picture had turned out so well?

She put it under her pillow and went to bed. She lay on her stomach, face into the pillow. Feeling a bit silly—but who'd ever know?—she whispered under her breath, invoking the emerald's magic, "Get me to Twiford tomorrow!"

Then she thought, But it should rhyme. So she added, "Make it a happy day, not full of sorrow." Then she went to sleep.

But a few hours later, she woke up with the feeling, There's something important I forgot to do. She turned the light on and picked up the phone.

"Hi, Mr. Fitzsimmons?" She was glad it was he, not some other night clerk she didn't know. "How are you? How's Nelson?"

"We're very well indeed, thanks. And you, Miss Hurnthile?"

"Fine too. I was just wondering, could you tell me what train I'd take if I wanted to go to Twiford, Surrey?"

"Surrey—that would be from Waterloo Station, I believe. I'll check the timetable, just a moment. Yes, Waterloo it is. You'd go to Wickham and from there you'd take a bus on to Twiford. Trains go twice an hour, at eleven minutes past the hour and fifty-three minutes past the hour. Return trains go on the hour and forty-two minutes past the hour."

"Wait a second, please, Mr. Fitzsimmons, I want to write that down." Jenny got out of bed and reached for the nearest things to write with. "11:11 or 11:53 from Waterloo," she jotted down in green pastel on the back of the sketch pad. "Okay, I've got it now, Mr. Fitzsimmons. How long is the ride?"

"An hour and five minutes on the train, ten minutes or so by bus."

"Thanks a lot."

"That's quite all right, Miss Hurnthile. Is there anything else I can find out for you?"

"I don't think so, thanks."

"Good night, then."

"Good night."

Twelve

Birds twittering in the courtyard and a nearby church bell woke Jenny at seven o'clock Friday morning. She swung her legs out of bed. But before her feet touched the floor, she swung her legs back in, and out again the other, the right side, of bed. And she decided, I'll make today a good day, no matter what.

She took the picture of the emerald out from under her pillow, so the chambermaid wouldn't wonder what it was doing there. It was a little wrinkled. She smoothed it out and put it in the desk drawer.

She took a shower. Then she put on the blue knit pants and the red-and-blue sweater she had worn on the plane, as a silent hint to her parents, Look, I'm wearing my traveling outfit.

"Better take your raincoat," Mom said before they went down to breakfast. It was sunny out, but yesterday had started sunny too and ended up raining. "And bring your guidebook, so we can read about Bermondsey on the way."

A Kids' Guide to London recommended it highly.

> Are you looking for a fine old china chamber pot, or shaving mug, or coffee mill, or ashtray shaped like a mermaid, or perhaps a combination penknife, corkscrew, nail clippers, nail file, and moustache comb as souvenirs or gifts? If so, don't miss the New Caledonian Market at Bermondsey Square, not far from the Tower Bridge, across the Thames in Southwark.

"That sounds like fun," said Mom on the bus, sitting next to Jenny, reading over her shoulder.

"Yes, it does," said Jenny, wishing like anything they were going to Twiford instead.

But when they got there, Jenny was soon caught up in the bustle and excitement. There were rows and rows of stands and stalls heaped high with all sorts of bric-a-brac and junk. "Look, Mom," she called, "I already found a present for Nancy!" It was a blue velvet drawstring bag with stars embroidered on it. "It's very different, she'll be the only kid in our class who has one, and it's just the right size for jacks. Should I get it?"

It cost one pound fifty. "It's worth that," said Mom. Jenny bought it.

Then Mom found something she couldn't resist: a bronze statuette, meant to be a paperweight, of a walrus with a luxuriant moustache and a quizzical, polite expression. "Doesn't this remind you of—?"

"Silverman!" said Jenny and Daddy in the same breath. There really was a striking resemblance. Mom and Daddy thought he would like it, and they bought it for him.

"Now let's find something for Trudl," said Mom.

They looked from stand to stand. Jenny found a good toy for Apricot Jones: a ball made of red plush, enclosed by shiny wires, with something inside that squeaked like a mouse when you moved it. She bought that too. It only cost fifty pence.

Meantime Mom had discovered a little round silver box that she loved. It stood on delicate curved silver legs and had a raised silver rose on the lid. The inside was lined with white velvet. Daddy bought it for her, and she was very pleased.

"We still don't have anything for Trudl," he said, looking at a crystal inkwell. "Do you think she'd like this for her desk?"

"There's no room on her desk," Jenny said. "Besides, she only uses cartridge and ball-point pens."

"Then how about this for her couch?" Mom examined an embroidered cushion.

"No, Mom, she already has twenty-three cushions."

"Okay, then *you* find something she'd like, Jenny," her father said.

Some pigeons whirred up from the sidewalk just

then. "A feather," Jenny remembered Aunt Trudl saying, "a jet-black feather freshly plucked from a raven's wing . . . a sidewalk picture." That made her think of the garden again and wish she were there, not here.

Her parents rummaged through trays of lockets and pins; old medals on faded ribbons; combs and big old hairpins of real and false tortoise shell; old spotted mirrors that looked as if they had chicken pox; tea cozies; antimacassars; stacks of old scratched records; and boxes of prints and engravings.

"There's nothing there for Aunt Trudl," said Jenny, looking down, discouraged. Then she saw an old fruit crate sticking out from under the stall. She crouched down to see what was in it: two filthy dilapidated dolls. One had thin, matted hair, gray with dust, and a broken eyelid, and a grimy, torn dress. The other had brown painted-on hair, but most of the paint had chipped off, and cracked cheeks, and no dress or pants on, so you could not tell if it was supposed to be a boy or girl.

Jenny turned her eyes away and stood up. Those dolls made her feel terrible. They gave off such a hopelessness, it was hard to imagine that they could ever have belonged to anybody and that anybody could ever have cared about them.

"Frankly, I've had about enough antiquing," Daddy said.

"Me too," Jenny agreed.

"Well, if we left now, there's a sculpture exhibit at the Tate I've been wanting to see," said Mom. "And you two could still catch the eleven eleven—"

Jenny couldn't believe she had heard right. "What did you say?"

"I said, you and Daddy could still catch the eleven eleven." She and Daddy smiled like two conspirators.

"You mean, from Waterloo?"

They nodded.

"To Twiford?" Jenny's voice went from small to almost yelling, "Are we going there?"

"Mm hm. You and I are," said Daddy. "If you still want to."

"Sure I do, you know I do, and how!"

"Come on, then. There's our bus."

The emerald's doing what I told it to! I conjured up its powers! It's starting to work! thought Jenny exuberantly as they ran to catch the bus.

On the ride to Waterloo her father took out a schedule of trains to and from Surrey and studied it.

"Daddy, where did you get that?"

"From a certain friend of yours, when we came back from the party last night."

"Mr. Fitzsimmons?"

"None other. He seemed to think we were planning on going to Twiford today. I wonder how he got that idea?" Daddy laughed and gave Jenny's shoulder a squeeze.

"Two round-trip tickets to Wickham, please,"

he said to the man behind the ticket window at Waterloo Station.

Walking with her parents to the platform where the train would be, Jenny asked them, "What made you change your minds?"

"The idea of you calling down to Mr. Fitzsimmons in the middle of the night to find out about train schedules to Twiford," Daddy answered. "That was such an enterprising thing to do, it impressed me a lot more than all your carrying on yesterday about how much you wanted to go."

"What did it for me was that picture you made of the garden," said Mom, "how hard you worked on it."

"You should see the picture I made after you left," said Jenny, with a secret, to-herself kind of smile.

"I'd like to. What is it of?"

"I'll show it to you some time," Jenny said. Let them think what they wanted about what had made them change their minds. She had her own idea what it was. Thank you, Emerald, she thought, more and more believing in its magic.

The train was already at the platform.

"I imagine we'll be back by eight at the latest," Daddy said to Mom. "Let's meet back at the hotel." He and Mom kissed good-bye.

Jenny climbed the first iron step leading up into the train. And she thought about Trudl, at the train station in Vienna, going up steps like this, by herself.

"Mom—!" Jenny turned around to her. She and Mom kissed.

Mom said, "I hope that whatever you expect of Twiford, you won't be disappointed."

"Thanks, Mom." Jenny hung on tight to her for a second. " 'Bye."

Thirteen

They had a whole compartment to themselves.
Jenny chose the window seat that faced backward.

"Are you sure you won't mind riding backward?" Daddy asked.

"I want to," she said, thinking, It'll make me
feel more as though I'm riding backward into
time. For that was how she thought of this trip.
"How old do you guess this train is, Daddy?"

"Pretty old. Why?"

"I was just wondering if it could be the same
train Aunt Trudl was on when she went to Twiford."

"Thirty-seven years ago? Let's hope it's a little
newer than that!"

Daddy unfolded his copy of the London *Times*.
But instead of reading, he asked, "Do you suppose you could explain to me now why we're
going to Twiford?"

Jenny's hand went to her mouth. She bit two
fingernails at once.

He reached across and took her hand. "Okay, I get the hint. I'll try not to be nosy. But could you just tell me, where do you figure we'll go when we get there? What are you planning we'll do?"

Instead of looking at him, Jenny looked out the window at the backyards of the outskirts of London. They were neat rectangles, dotted red, white, yellow, pink, and blue with spring flowers. "When we get there," she answered, looking out the window, "we'll go to the garden." She adjusted it in her mind from summer to now. Instead of roses and all those summer flowers, it would have tulips, crocuses, daffodils, hyacinths, and those little blue ones that looked like stars. And the leaves on the trees would still be fresh, and the grass would still look new . . .

"Hey, come back!" Daddy tapped her on the knee. "To what garden will we go?"

"To the one in front of the house of the people Aunt Trudl stayed with."

"How will we find it?"

"I know the address."

"Well, that's something. And what'll we do there?"

"Don't worry, Daddy." Jenny closed her eyes and leaned her head back against the soft, upholstered back rest. She listened to the chug-a-chug rhythm of the wheels on the tracks. It lulled her. It made her feel peaceful. After a while the rhythm seemed to have words to it, chug-chanting: "The emerald's getting you there/Getting you there/Getting you there." With every repetition, she believed it more. "The magic will make you know what to do/What to do. . . . The magic is working/Is working. . . ."

So lulled, Jenny dropped into sleep, even though it was still only morning. And she missed seeing the outskirts of London change to country-side.

At 12:15 the train arrived at Wickham. A small green bus marked "Twiford" stood waiting at the station.

The ride was through gently sloping meadows, past woods and newly plowed fields separated by hedgerows. Here and there stood cows and sheep. It felt as though they were much farther away from London than only an hour and ten minutes.

For the last few minutes of the ride, the road ran alongside a green, slow-flowing river.

"That's the river Mark caught frogs in," said Jenny.

"Who is Mark?"

"Mark Sanderson, the boy of the people Aunt Trudl stayed with. Look, Daddy, there's Twi-ford!"

The road and river parted. Roofs, chimneys, and a square church tower came into view. "In a minute you'll see the Stirrup Cup, that's the pub where the bus'll stop," Jenny said.

"Hm." Daddy gave her a searching look. "You said Aunt Trudl didn't tell you much about this place. Then how do you know so much about it?"

117

"I don't know that much. Besides, you said you wouldn't be nosy."

"Okay, I withdraw the question. Say, that Stirrup Cup place looks inviting." The bus had stopped in front of it, the door to it was open. You could see people inside, standing around eating sandwiches, drinking beer. "I don't think kids are supposed to go into pubs. But how about if I brought us out some ginger beers and sandwiches? It's just about lunchtime. I'm starved."

"No, please!" With one hand, Jenny pulled him on, while at her other hand—so it seemed to her— the power of the emerald pulled mightily, pulled her to the garden.

"Take it easy! Where are you dragging me to?"

"Sutpin Lane. Number Seventeen."

"Do you know how to get there?"

"Not exactly. But if we just start walking—"

Daddy asked the bus driver, who was just about to go into the pub, "Excuse me, could you tell us how to get to Sutpin Lane?"

The driver mumbled something with his mouth almost closed, "Mumble you mumble mumble States?"

It sounded as though he were asking if they were from the United States. Daddy said, "Yes, we are."

The driver answered, not more distinctly, but pointing with his hand, which helped, "Down High, to Church, and there you'll mumble mumble Sut—mn—mm."

"I see. Thanks very much. Hey, Jenny, wait for me!"

She was halfway down the block. Her father had to run to catch up to her. "Can't we enjoy the scenery while we're here? Look at these old cobblestones. And those houses with the beams and the top stories sticking out are Tudor, the real thing, not imitations. They've stood here for four hundred years."

Jenny gave them a quick glance without slowing down.

Among the stores they passed was a place called Cumberwell's Teas, with cakes, iced and plain, and fresh-baked loaves of bread in the window. "I'm really ready for a bite of lunch," Daddy said.

"First let's go to Sutpin Lane, please!" She pulled him on. They came to the church they had seen from the distance. It was built of gray stone and had a square, squat tower with ivy growing over it.

They turned into Church Street. It was a pleasant country-town street with trees and comfortable-looking houses with well-kept front lawns. Jenny ran till she came to a side street leading off it. "There's Sutpin Lane!"

Sutpin Lane started out looking like the same kind of street, tree-lined, with one-family houses with front lawns and hedges and gardens in the back into which you could not see.

"What number did you say, Jen?"

"Seventeen." She could see it in her mind's eye,

written on the copybook's first page, small and neat with a line through the seven, the way Europeans write it.

But the last house was Number Eleven. There the lane ended. There, on tall wooden posts, stood a large sign proclaiming "Sutpin Estates."

Beyond the sign, for as far as one could see, were brown and white two-story houses, in clusters of four, around eighty altogether, maybe more. They all looked the same. They were not old, but already looked shabby, needing fresh paint. They had staircases on the outside. They had small windows and the upper stories had tiny balconies. On some of those balconies stood baby carriages and tricycles and scooters. In between the houses were parking lots with cars, and in between the parking lots were bits of lawn with clothes driers shaped like trees, and some real trees, spindly and new, and here and there some seesaws and swings.

" 'Estates!' That's what the driver was asking, were we looking for 'Sutpin Estates,' " Daddy said.

Jenny's face had turned almost as white as the shirt under her sweater. She couldn't swallow. She felt knotted up inside with raging disappointment. She thought, The emerald tricked me! It got me here for nothing!

"What'll we do now?" Daddy asked.

"Nothing." She said it so bitterly, Daddy tilted her face up and tried to comfort her. "Sweetheart, it isn't the end of the world. What did you think—that everything would have stayed exactly the same as when Trudl lived here?"

"I don't know—"

Daddy put his raincoat on. "Look what's happening to the sky!"

Wind had blown the clouds together into thick, threatening grayness overhead. A sudden strong gust whipped and billowed the diapers and clothes hanging out to dry. It blew Jenny's hair into her face.

She stood there letting strands of it be blown over her eyes.

Daddy tucked the hair back behind her ears. "I, for one, have looked my fill at the splendors of Sutpin Estates," he said, trying to joke. "Come on, where to now?"

"Back to the bus. Back to London."

"After coming all this way? Jenny, you can't mean that!"

"I do."

"In that case, I'm disappointed in you. I gave you credit for having sense, I thought you knew what you were doing."

Rain came down, hard. Jenny didn't care if she got wet or not.

Her father threw her raincoat over her. He was angry now, and yelled, "What's the matter with you, anyway?"

Just then there was a lightning flash. It seemed to tear the sky in two. Jenny stared straight up at it. It blinded her for a moment. She shut her eyes. The after-image of the lightning blazed on the insides of her eyelids. In the interval before the thunderclap, she thought of the Devil—had he come down in a blaze like that, when he fell out of the sky?

Fourteen

Her father ran, pulling Jenny along, to the nearest place of shelter, the church.

"No, I don't want to go in there!"

"Why not? Anybody can go into a church, you know. Not just Christians. Not even just people who believe in God."

Her father didn't, Jenny knew. The last time they had talked about it, Jenny hadn't either. But now she didn't know any more what she believed in.

Daddy pushed open the heavy oak door. It was cool and dark inside and no one was there.

"You're shaking," said Daddy. "Come, let's sit down." They went into a pew toward the back. "Now, Jenny, pull yourself together. There's nothing to be so upset about." To show that he wasn't angry any more, he put his hand on top of hers. But she pulled her hand out from under his and bit at her nails, one after the other, thinking, If there is a God, even if He doesn't care who comes in here, He'd draw the line at somebody who be-

lieves in things like emeralds with evil powers
from His one big enemy.

And believe in it she did, more than ever. Yes, it
had gotten her here, with its evil magic, and it was
making the day just awful.

Thunder rumbled all around, as if God were
agreeing, Yes, He drew the line.

"Daddy, let's get out of here!"

"Wait just a little, till the rain lets up."

They sat there for what seemed like ages. Jenny
imagined it being Sunday, and a minister preach-
ing from the pulpit, and the pews filled with people in old-fashioned clothes, and Trudl sitting
here, thinking about the goldfish rotting in the
ground. She imagined music coming out of the or-
gan pipes and the people in the pews standing up
to sing. There was a hymn book in a pouch on the
back of the pew in front. Jenny took it out of
there. "Let it open to 'All Things Bright and Beautiful,'" she implored, she didn't know to whom.
And she let it fall open in her lap. It opened to
some other hymn. She took this as a signal that
nothing—NOTHING!—would come right for her.

The hammering of the rain let up. "Okay, I
think we can go now," her father said and guided
her to the door.

Outside, in the daylight, he looked her in the
face. "Jenny, do you feel sick?" he asked. "You
look kind of greenish."

Her stomach jumped with dread. She imagined
herself with a greenish face forever, as a sign to

one and all, "I am under the emerald's curse. . . ."

"Yes, I feel sick." She gave a retching cough. "I may throw up."

"No, you won't. Just take deep breaths. You'll be okay once you get some food inside you. We haven't had a thing to eat since seven o'clock, and it's a quarter past two."

He rushed her back to Cumberwell's. There he ordered tea and brown bread. It came with butter, and apricot and gooseberry jam. After the first bite, Jenny realized she was starved. She ate four slices, then started on some raisin cake.

"There. I can see you're feeling better." Daddy leaned over the table, closer to her. "Let's talk sensibly now. Tell me, if Number Seventeen had still been there, and we'd gone into the garden, someone would have asked what we were doing there, right? And we'd have asked if the people Trudl stayed with still lived there—what was their name again?"

"Sanderson."

"Okay, and if they still lived there, we'd have gone in the house and talked with them, right?"

"Yes."

"Well, then, it's obvious what we have to do: find out if any Sandersons still live in Twiford. If so, we'll go see them, all right?"

"I guess so."

"Finish your cake." Her father got up and asked the lady behind the counter if he could see the telephone directory.

"Here you are, sir." She handed him one.

Jenny had a hunch he wouldn't find any Sandersons listed. In fact, she hoped he wouldn't. She did not want to go into a strange house that had nothing to do with the garden—into a house where Trudl had never set foot. She did not want to talk to strangers who probably had never known Trudl, and if they had, would not remember her.

"Are you sure they don't spell it with a *u?*" Daddy called.

"I'm sure."

"Well, I can't find any Sandersons, which is odd, because that's a fairly common name."

"I knew you wouldn't," said Jenny.

"Ridiculous. You couldn't have known." Daddy asked the lady behind the counter if she knew anyone thereabouts by that name.

She was sorry, she did not.

"You see? It's no use," Jenny said.

Once they had left the tea shop, Jenny's father reproached her. "Why are you being so negative? Why are you acting as if this trip to Twiford—which was your idea—were doomed?"

She was glad that *he* had said the word. "Because it is," she answered.

"Baloney!" Daddy said so loud, a passer-by shook his head at the strange expression. "What if I decided in the middle of a trial, 'this trial's doomed,' and used that as an excuse to do a lousy job defending some innocent client, and he ended up in jail?"

"That's different, Daddy."

"Not at all. People have to take responsibility for what they do. That's one thing I believe in. So does Mom. We've tried to bring you up that way."

"I know."

"Well, then, live up to it. You wanted to come here. I didn't make you tell me why—"

Jenny didn't want him to get mad again. "I'd tell you if I could, Daddy."

"Well, if you can't, you can't. Some things are private, I understand that. But I couldn't help figuring this much out: You're feeling awfully guilty about something. It has to do with Aunt Trudl. And the reason we're here is so you can make amends somehow. The trouble is, you don't know how, do you?"

She shook her head.

"Well, one way would be to have something more to tell her about Twiford than just that the house she lived in is gone. Don't you think so?"

"I guess so."

"Come on, then. We haven't seen half of this place yet. Let's explore a little. Who knows what we'll find?"

He took her hand. They walked down High Street. He admired the old houses, the neat shops, and how few cars went by. Jenny brooded what a gyp it was that those old houses should still be standing, but not the one on Sutpin Lane.

They passed a library, a post office, a school.

Jenny didn't know if Trudl had gone to any of these. Daddy insisted on going in, nevertheless.

Then the houses stood farther apart. The cobblestones ended. High Street became a country road, leading out toward hilly woodland and farmland.

"Let's head back toward the center," Daddy said. "Think, Jenny: Did Trudl ever mention any other people we could look up?"

"I can't think of any."

"Well, can you think of any special places—where she went swimming, or on picnics, or something—that we could look for, so at least we could tell her about those?"

"No."

He sighed, discouraged.

They had come to the edge of town. The road forked in two directions; in between was a formal triangle of lawn on which stood a war memorial: a statue of a soldier on a broad slab of marble with the dates 1939–1945 carved into it, and the names of men from Twiford who died in World War II.

One of the names was Sanderson, Robert Marcus, Lt. Col.

Jenny knew it was Mr. Sanderson, because of the "Marcus." Suddenly she saw him in her mind—a tall, reddish-haired man, not wearing a soldier's uniform, but a business suit. He had a kind face. She could almost hear him say, with a British accent, "What a pretty frock you have on," when he first saw Trudl in her poppy dress with the label pinned to it.

Daddy put his arm around her shoulders. "It could be some other Sanderson, you know."

"No, it was him."

They stood there like that a few moments. Then Daddy said sadly, "I guess we may as well head back to the bus."

Fifteen

"No, wait!" Jenny heard a clomping of hoofs in the distance. It got louder, it came nearer—"Horses!" A gray speckled one ridden by a man cantered into view, and one the color of chestnuts, ridden by a woman.

"I do know a place I'd like to see," said Jenny excitedly. "The riding stable!"

"Well, good, I'm glad you thought of something! Let's just make sure there *is* one. Those may be private horses, you know."

When the riders came nearer, Daddy asked them.

Yes, they said, there was an excellent riding stable, Harwood's. "Take this road till you come to another fork," the man on the gray horse directed them. "Bear left to the river. Cross the bridge and there you are."

The weather had turned sunny and cooler. Daddy started to say, "Who'd have thought an hour ago that we'd be taking a nice afternoon

stroll—hey, Jenny!" She was far ahead, running—
like the wind, I'm running like the wind, she
thought, wind whistling in her ears.

The road narrowed into a footpath and led
through a meadow full of tiny white, yellow, and
blue flowers. Jenny imagined the brightness
away, she imagined it nighttime, and Trudl in her
"nightdress," and Felicity Emma, very alive, and
Ballou, with wild, happy yips, all running to the
stable.

At the bridge she stopped and waited for her
father.

They crossed it together. On the other side a
meadow sloped upward from the bank toward a
small orchard of trees with white blossoms. Beyond those stood a house and a barn. Outside the
barn was a car, some bicycles, and a truck with a
horse-trailer. To the right was a long, low building, the stable. Behind it the land sloped still
higher, and at the crest of the slope, outlined
against the sky, three horses stood grazing. Jenny
thought some day she'd try to sketch the view
from here from memory. "Isn't it beautiful,
Daddy?"

"It certainly is. But you know, I didn't even
know Trudl used to ride. You'd think she would
have told me. Did she ride a lot, do you know?"

Jenny shook her head. She wondered what he'd
say if he knew that Trudl really only rode in that
story she made up.

"Well, don't be disappointed if this turns out not to be the place. There may have been another stable in those days."

"I know. It doesn't matter. I just really want to see the horses."

"Okay. I'm surprised though, Jenny. I didn't know you liked horses that much."

"I'm just starting to." As Jenny said this, she had a vivid picture of a horse like Midnight in her mind.

When they reached the orchard, they could see behind the barn. There was a fenced-in riding ring, and a lesson going on. Four riders—three girls near Jenny's age, and a boy, younger—trotted around, posting up and down. Two horses were chestnut brown; one was tan; and the boy rode a dark brown, rather fat pony. A teacher stood in the middle, calling out instructions.

As Jenny and her father approached the ring, a gray-haired man came toward them down the hill, leading one of the horses—a white one—that had been grazing up there. "May I help you?" he asked. "Did you want to inquire about riding with us?"

"No. I hope we're not intruding," Jenny's father said. "We'd just like to look around at the horses, if it's all right."

"By all means. Start with this one, go on, pat her if you like," the man invited Jenny. "Her name is Starlight, though I'm afraid she's a bit muddy just now."

132

Jenny touched her on the cheek. It felt wonderfully silky.

"Look around, by all means. Excuse me, I must see that Starlight gets cleaned up. Good-bye." He smiled at them and led the mare off to the stable.

Jenny and her father went up to the ring.

The pupils in there all wore riding breeches, riding jackets, and round riding hats with visors.

The teacher had jeans, a sweater, and a riding hat on. She faced away from Jenny and her father. "Keep those heads up! Heels down! Knees in!" she called. "Now let me see you posting. Giddy-yap!"

The horses speeded up to a trot. The riders posted as best they could. This meant they rose up and down in the stirrups in rhythm with the horses' movements in order to avoid getting bounced around in the saddle. "No, Elizabeth, not like that!" The girl named Elizabeth was having so much trouble, the teacher asked her to dismount. Then she swung herself up onto Elizabeth's horse, and with perfect posture and rhythm demonstrated how to post. She did it so well, she made it seem easy.

When she came around the curve of the ring, she caught sight of Jenny and her father.

"Look how she's looking at us," Jenny whispered. "I bet she doesn't like people watching her lessons. That man should have told us not to stand here. Daddy, let's go."

"We can't, now. That wouldn't be polite."

133

The teacher had dismounted and returned the horse to Elizabeth. "Walk your horses around the ring. I'll be back in a moment," she said to the class.

She came toward Jenny and her father. She carried herself very straight. She had a weather-beaten face with many wrinkles, but firm cheeks and a not-droopy chin. She had wide-apart eyes which, all the while she came nearer, looked intently at them both, though more at Jenny than her father.

She looks mad about something, Jenny thought.

Her father cleared his throat. "Ahem, I'm afraid we've disrupted your lesson."

"That's quite all right." She sounded as though she weren't thinking about that at all. And she stared at them.

Inside the ring the pony suddenly gave an angry snort. "Timothy, how many times have I told you, don't rein him in so hard!" the teacher shouted. Abruptly she dismissed the class: "That's all for today. We'll have a longer lesson next time."

They dismounted and led the horses toward the barn.

She turned back to Jenny and her father. "You must be from America," she said in a very different voice. "Oh, dear, I'm sure you think me very rude for staring—I'm still doing it! I can't seem to be able to help it." She gave a little laugh. Below the laugh, her voice shook. Perhaps to give her hands something to do, she took off her riding hat. Her hair had been tucked under it. Now it came down in a single braid, thick and gray. It bounced against her shoulder. She flipped it back, all the while keeping her eyes fixed on Jenny's face.

Usually when someone stares, the other person turns away. But something about this woman's eyes held Jenny's. Her eyes were fiery brown. That kind of brown goes with red hair, even though she's got gray hair now, Jenny thought.

Just then the woman said, "You look astonishingly like somebody I once knew."

This can't be happening, thought Jenny, feeling hot, cold, and shivery. And her mouth felt so dry, and her tongue felt like such a jelly blob, she was sure her tongue couldn't form, or her lips let out what she thought. So it was as though someone else were saying it, when she heard herself say, "I look like Trudl. And you're Pam."

A dog came bounding over from the barn. He barked. He sniffed at Jenny's father. He put his paws on Jenny's shoulders and licked her face. His paws had real mud on them, his tongue felt wet, he smelled of real dog. So she knew this was all really happening.

"Rufus, behave yourself," said the woman, her voice not shaking any more. She held one hand out to Jenny, one to Jenny's father. "Yes, I'm Pam. Pamela Harwood, now."

They shook her hands.

"I'm Harry Ehrenteil, Trudl's brother, and this is my daughter, Jenny."

"How do you do, how do you do—" Jenny said, thinking, Of all the dumb things to say! It doesn't say anything about how anybody's feeling.

But she could tell from Pam's—Mrs. Harwood's—face that she was feeling a whole lot more than you'd expect, if all you knew about her was what was in the copybook.

Daddy looked really surprised and glad, but kind of embarrassed, too, and didn't know what to say next.

"And me, I feel so—so—" Jenny could not put it in words. The knots inside had all loosened up. She felt like hugging this whole place, including the horses, like hugging the day for the way it was turning out. She riffled her fingers through Rufus's long wavy fur. She asked, "Does he look anything like Ballou?"

"He does, a little." Mrs. Harwood sounded glad that Jenny knew about Ballou. "Ken!" she called to the gray-haired man coming out of the stable. "Come and meet our visitors! This is my husband, Ken. Ken, this is Mr. Ehrenteil, from America, imagine, Trudl's brother! And this is Jenny, Trudl's niece. You know, when I first saw her standing there, outside the ring, I thought my eyes were playing tricks on me, I thought it was Trudl—"

"How do you do, what a pleasure this is!" Mr.

Harwood shook hands with Jenny and her father. With his other hand he took a handkerchief out. "Here, Pam."

She blew her nose, snorting almost as loud as the pony had done.

Sixteen

They went into the house, into a room with comfortable furniture, bookcases, and lots of pictures on the walls, mostly of horses and hunting scenes, and logs and kindling prepared in the fireplace. Mr. Harwood lit the fire.

"Mr. Ehrenteil, do sit here." Mrs. Harwood offered him a wing chair with a footstool for his feet. "And Jenny, you here." She showed Jenny to a window seat. It was near the fire and had a view out on the hill where two of the horses still grazed. "And this is Bianca." She introduced a long-haired white cat in the corner. Bianca let Jenny take her in her lap, and purred when Jenny stroked her, adding to how much Jenny already felt at home here.

The grown-ups were not so at ease. Mrs. Harwood said she really ought to go and put the kettle on.

"No, please don't trouble," said Jenny's father, "at least not on our account. We had tea a short while ago."

"Then you must have some sherry," said Mr. Harwood, but the cork seemed to be stuck. Finally he got it out. He poured sherry for the grown-ups, and for Jenny ginger beer. Mrs. Harwood passed around a plate of "biscuits" three times though no one wanted any. Then no one could think what to say first.

"Come in, Rufus," Mrs. Harwood called, relieved to be able to break the silence. She let in the dog who'd been scratching at the door. The cat stayed unruffled at the sight of him. He lay down by the fire.

Mrs. Harwood paced around, looking from Jenny's father to Jenny, and said, "I simply can't believe it!"

"Do sit down, dear," said her husband.

But instead she came over to Jenny, cupped Jenny's face in her hands, and looked at her some more—which, amazingly, did not embarrass Jenny. They ended up smiling.

Then Mrs. Harwood sat down in a chair next to Jenny's father. "How ever did you find us?" she asked.

"We very nearly didn't," he said. "We nearly gave up and went back to London. We started out at Sutpin Lane, you see."

They talked about Sutpin Estates. Mrs. Harwood said those houses were frightful. She told about her mother selling their old house ages ago, after the war, after her father died.

"We're so sorry," Jenny's father put in. "We saw

the memorial. In fact it was there Jenny got the idea—quite out of the blue—she wanted to see the riding stable."

"A jolly good idea," said Mr. Harwood, pouring her more ginger beer.

Mrs. Harwood said, now that they'd found their way here, they'd stay, wouldn't they, at least the weekend?

Daddy explained they couldn't because Mom expected them back tonight and because they were leaving for home the day after tomorrow.

How *did* we find our way? Jenny wondered to herself, sipping ginger beer. How *did* I get the idea I wanted to see the stable? Not "out of the blue." Out of the copybook. She steeled herself against the guilt that always came over her when she thought about that. But it did not come. On the contrary. She continued feeling wonderful. The fire flames leaped before her like dancers; the ginger beer bubbles fizzed deliciously against her tongue; Bianca purred on in her lap. She almost had to laugh out loud, remembering that just a short while ago she had thought this trip was doomed. The emerald flashed into her mind. I owe it an apology, she thought. It didn't trick me. It didn't get me here for nothing!

The grown-ups' conversation, meantime, had gotten around to Trudl. Mrs. Harwood said, "I've wondered so often, what is she like? What sort of life has she led? Is she well? Is she happy?"

Jenny's father seemed to think those were hard

questions to answer. He cleared his throat several times. "Let's see, where shall I start? Trudl graduated from college in 1948. She got married in '51, and divorced after eight or nine years. Then she went back to school and did graduate work in comparative literature. She lives alone, in the same apartment house we do. She works as a translator—Jenny, help me out!" He laughed apologetically. "I've made her life sound like something a computer might type out on one of those cards full of little holes. You try, you'll do better."

"Aunt Trudl's life isn't full of holes! Her life is fine," said Jenny. "It's kind of different from most people's. But it's exactly how she likes it. She doesn't live alone, she has two cats of hers, and one of mine, and a turtle of mine that live in her apartment. She likes what she does for her work as much as the things she does for fun. And she could get married again, she'd just rather not. The only hole might be, she hasn't got children—I mean, of her own. But she's got me. She and I are really close."

"That's good, then she's not lonely. It *was* rather a lonely time for her when she stayed with us. And Mark and I didn't make it easy for her. As a matter of fact, I remember being rather beastly to Trudl. . . ."

She sounded so sad that Jenny blurted out, to make her feel better, "I know, but you're a lot nicer now."

An embarrassed silence followed. Jenny realized

she might as well have said, "That's right, you were beastly to her."

Her father said, "Ahem," again. "Jenny didn't mean—"

Jenny quickly said, "I'm sorry."

"There's no need to be sorry," said Mrs. Harwood. "It's quite true, I *am* nicer now."

"Well, so's Aunt Trudl," said Jenny. "She was awful then, too. She told me so."

Then everybody laughed and felt relieved.

Mrs. Harwood started telling about her family. Mark was a naval architect, living in Bognor Regis, by the sea, with his wife and three children of whom two were grown up and the youngest was ten. Mrs. Sanderson lived there too. She was eighty-three years old but in good health. "I wish you could meet them, Jenny. And our two daughters, Margaret and Jill. Jill's at college, Margaret's married. We do have some photographs. I'll fetch them down. Come with me, Jenny, if you like."

They went upstairs.

"Here we are, this is where we sleep."

Jenny followed Mrs. Harwood into a room with flowered wallpaper and dormer windows and a large brass bed and old-fashioned lamps.

"The photographs are in here somewhere." Mrs. Harwood opened a door and disappeared into a dark storage attic.

Jenny heard her shifting boxes and cartons around in there. A nose-tantalizing, musky smell seeped out into the room. "Mrs. Harwood, can I help you look?"

"I'd rather you didn't, Jenny. It's awfully messy, and there's been a sudden mouse population explosion. I must speak to Bianca about that."

Finally she came out of there. In one hand she carried a box of photographs. Under her other arm she carried a doll.

The doll had green eyes. They seemed to look straight at Jenny, as though she knew her.

Jenny's heart did a flip-flop.

"Felicity-Emma!"

Yes, yes, it was she, it couldn't be another doll, Jenny knew for sure. But how come, how could that be? What about that night when Pam got so sick and threw up, and what about her promise to Trudl?

While Jenny thought about that, she suddenly had the feeling, That's what Mrs. Harwood's thinking about, too. . . .

Mrs. Harwood, avoiding Jenny's eyes, plucked a cobweb from the doll's honey-colored hair. She wiped dirt off her porcelain cheek and whisked a bit of dust off her dress. Then she put her into Jenny's arms.

"I want you to take her to America with you. Will you do that, Jenny?" she asked. Her rust-brown eyes were full on Jenny's face now. From the look in them, Jenny knew why Mrs. Harwood was giving her Felicity-Emma: not so much as a gift—Mrs. Harwood could see Jenny was almost

too old for dolls—but because she was thinking
about that promise.

Promises do get broken sometimes, I know
about that, Jenny thought. "Yes, I will," she answered in a hushed voice, earnestly. "I'd love to.
Thanks, Mrs. Harwood. Thanks, really, a lot."

Then she glanced down at Felicity-Emma's face.
The doll's green eyes were almost smiling, as
though she'd heard everything, and was glad.

"That's quite all right." Mrs. Harwood sounded
much happier. "Now tell me something, Jenny.
How is it you called her Felicity-*Emma*?"

Jenny hadn't realized she had said that name
out loud. "Because—well—Aunt Trudl called her
that, but in secret. I shouldn't have told."

"Oh, I dare say Trudl would not object to my
finding out now. Some secrets get less secret with
time, don't you think? Felicity-*Emma*—" she
mulled over the name "—Em-ma—I say! I wonder
if that could have anything to do with that ring
she had, with the em—"

"No!" said Jenny, eager to stop her. "I think
some secrets get *more* secret." And even as she
said that, she had the oddest, "seecretest" feeling—making her tingle all over with anticipation—
that the emerald was near, perhaps in this very
room.

"Pam!" called Mr. Harwood up the stairs.
"Hadn't you and Jenny better come down soon?
Or there won't be enough time to show Jenny and
her father around the place!"

144

"We're coming," Mrs. Harwood called back. They left that room and went down. But the feeling of the emerald being nearby remained with Jenny.

Her father gave her a surprised look when he saw the doll she was holding.

"Mrs. Harwood gave her to me," Jenny said.

"That's very kind of you, Mrs. Harwood, but are you quite sure you want Jenny to—?"

"Quite sure," Mrs. Harwood answered before he'd finished the question. "Now, let me show you these photographs."

There were some of Mr. and Mrs. Sanderson, and of Pam and Mark when they were small. There were some of Number Seventeen Sutpin Lane, and some, though not too clear, of the garden. There was one of Ballou. There was one of Pam riding Midnight; one of Mark and another boy wading in the river; and one of Pam and Mark and Trudl in Sunday clothes. Trudl in her poppy dress. Then came some of Mark and Pam, older, then some of Mr. Harwood, and of Mark's wife, and Mark's children (one of them holding Nirob!), and of Margaret and Jill.

Then the Harwoods showed Jenny and her father around. Rufus came along. Jenny touched most of the fourteen horses in the stable on their silky faces. She learned not to stand within kicking range behind them. Mrs. Harwood held up one horse's foot for her to see how the horseshoe fitted onto the hoof. Mr. Harwood had some

lumps of sugar in his pockets. He gave them to
Jenny to feed to the horses. He told her their
names and which was the fastest, which had won
the most ribbons, which had been sick, which was
quick-tempered, which the most affectionate. And
she saw for herself which was Mrs. Harwood's favorite: a sleek, black horse with soft, brown eyes
named Jet Princess who differed from Midnight
only in that her white fleck was on her chest, instead of on her forehead.

When they finished the tour of the stables, Jenny's father said, "Now I'm afraid we must get the
bus to Wickham."

The Harwoods would not hear of them taking
the bus. They drove them to Wickham themselves
and waited there with them until the train came.

After they said good-bye and exchanged ad-
dresses and promised to keep in touch, Mrs. Harwood pulled Jenny close and said, "Give my love
to Trudl. And Jenny, tell her—oh, but you'll know
yourself what to tell her from me." She put her
lips against Jenny's cheek in a quick kiss of good-
bye. Then she blew her nose again with an un-
abashedly loud snort.

Seventeen

"Well, I guess you knew when we started out this morning, Twiford was not tops on my list of places I wanted to go," said Jenny's father, settling into a corner of the train compartment. "Now I'll admit, I'm glad you made me come. I wouldn't have missed it for anything."

"I'm glad too," Jenny said.

"But I don't understand Mrs. Harwood giving you that doll. It seems like too much of a present. Besides, you don't even play with dolls much any more."

"I know. But you see—" Jenny explained that long ago Pam had promised her to Trudl and then not kept the promise.

"I see. Did Mrs. Harwood tell you all that?"

Jenny shook her head.

"Did Aunt Trudl?"

"No."

"Well, then how do you know?"

"I wish I could tell you, Daddy. But I can't. One of these days I'll be able to. Just not yet."

"Very well, question withdrawn," he said like a

lawyer; then he gave a loud, unlawyerly yawn. "Phew! It's been a big day. I'm exhausted."

"Wait, before you go to sleep, have you got a comb?"

He lent her one. Then he let his head sink onto his shoulder and dozed off.

There were no other people in the compartment. Jenny sat Felicity-Emma on her knee and started combing her hair, gingerly at first. But when she saw how firmly rooted it was, she combed it hard, till all the snarls and dust were out. Then she untucked her own white shirt out of the waistline of her pants; she wet the edge of the shirt with her tongue and used it as a washcloth on Felicity-Emma's face, neck, arms, legs, and hands and feet.

That's the best I can clean you up for now, she thought.

Then she leaned back in her seat and closed her eyes, putting aside how grown-up she was getting. She let her whole self enjoy the sensation of holding Felicity-Emma. And, in and around and behind that sensation was that other feeling, even stronger—about the emerald being near.

The wheels on the track took it up in rhythm: "The emerald is near, is near!" Then "near" changed to "here." "Is here," chanted the wheels, "the emerald is here!" Again and again they chanted it.

Tired though Jenny was, this time she did not let the chanting lull her to sleep. She sat up

148

straight in her seat. Here—where? How come? she asked herself, and told herself, I have to figure this out.

She went back in her mind to the last page she'd read in the copybook, where Trudl had written, with the emerald between her fingers, in "invisibel" handwriting, over Felicity-Emma's and Nirob's bodies, "Be alive forever . . ."

Well, that had worked, she knew, judging by how Felicity-Emma felt to her, and by the expression on Mark's kid's face in the photograph of him playing with Nirob. And then Trudl did that other, most secret of all thing, and said that rhyme, "From this day on, in darkness shine!"— Damn!

The train had ground to a halt. They were at a station. A couple with a baby came into the compartment, breaking Jenny's concentration.

The mother sat the baby on her lap. The baby was pretty fat, and a girl, you could tell by her sweater and crocheted hat being pink. The father took a banana out of one of the many bags they had with them. He peeled it. "Here's a bite for Mummy. Now one for Daddums," the mother crooned, stuffing banana bites in. They got mushed all over the baby's face.

Jenny turned away—and she had the answer, all of a sudden it was there! It seemed so obvious to her now, she couldn't imagine how she could *not* have known all this time.

Trudl, that August day, had sat just like a

mother with Felicity-Emma on her lap, and fed her—not so messily, not bites of banana—but the emerald.

And that's where it still is to this day, shining in darkness, inside Felicity-Emma, and nobody knew till now!

She lifted the doll up so her throat was level with Jenny's ear. She shook her. Thump, thump, thump, she heard—but that was her own heart, beating hard. Over that, plus the noise of the train, it was pretty impossible to hear the kind of tiny rattling a small emerald could make inside the doll.

But it's in there, it has to be, Jenny was sure. And the second line of the rhyme leaped into her mind: "Do no more harm. But still be mine!"

I'll get it out, I'll bring it back to Aunt Trudl, she thought excitedly. She couldn't wait to see the look on Aunt Trudl's face when Aunt Trudl saw the emerald again.

Back at the hotel, Mom was awfully glad to see them. She thought Felicity-Emma was beautiful. Over dinner they told about their day.

Afterward, in the stillness of her room, Jenny listened again to the doll's throat, and thought she heard a rattling—very, very faint—in there. And she thought, I'll try to take it out now.

She turned Felicity-Emma upside down and tapped her on the back of the neck, first lightly, then a little harder, then hard. Nothing happened.

She moved her nearer. She squeezed one eye

shut. With her other eye she peered into the doll's mouth. All she could see in there were two small upper teeth.

She tapped her one more hard tap. Still nothing. I need something to get at it with, she thought. Like a hatpin. Or a darning needle. Or a long hairpin. Maybe someone who stayed in this room before left one around somewhere. She searched. There were none in the bathroom cabinet. She opened all the drawers of the dressing table. And in the bottom left-hand drawer, underneath the paper lining, she found one.

She unbent it. She stuck it into Felicity-Emma's mouth and probed around. But it was no use. She could not do it.

She went to bed. But she was so excited and disappointed both, she didn't sleep soundly and kept waking up.

Her parents had gone out somewhere after dinner.

She woke up whenever the elevator door opened and closed. When her parents came back, she recognized their footsteps in the corridor.

"Mom, could you come in here a minute?"

Mom came in. "It's very late. Why aren't you asleep?"

"I was. Sit down, Mom. I want to show you something." She held Felicity-Emma up to Mom's ear. "Listen really hard." She shook the doll. "Do you hear that?"

"No."

"Well, it's very faint."

"What is?"

"She has something in her throat. I want to get it out. I tried with a hairpin. I couldn't. Do you think you could?"

"Can't it wait till morning?"

"Please, Mom, try now." Jenny gave her the hairpin. Mom tried. She couldn't do it either.

"What is it, anyway?" she asked. "Why does it have to come out in the middle of the night?"

"Because it's important! I can't tell you what it is, but you'll see! Please, Mom, try one more time."

"No. It's impossible. But I'll tell you what: I passed a place today where they might be able to get it out. We could go there tomorrow, if it's that important."

"What sort of place?"

"A doll hospital. Now go to sleep. Good night."

Eighteen

The doll hospital was a short bus ride away, in the Brompton Road. It was a small store crowded with dolls.

The owner was a stout woman with a gruff voice. She had horn-rimmed glasses and a tight permanent wave. She wore a white jacket over her dress.

Handing Felicity-Emma over, Jenny felt a little the way she had felt handing Apricot Jones to the veterinarian when she had to get her shots.

The doll-hospital owner examined Felicity-Emma from head to feet. Jenny could tell she admired how smoothly the eyelids worked, how unsqueakingly the head could be turned, and how readily, yet not too loosely, the arms and legs could be moved. "Hmmm," she muttered extra gruffly to conceal her eagerness. "How much are you asking for this doll?"

"No, you don't understand! She's not for sale! I brought her here because she has something in her throat. And I thought you could take it out."

"Does she now?" The woman shook her, not as gently as Jenny had done. "I can't hear anything."

"She does have something in there, though."

"We'll see about that." The woman took a pad and started to write a receipt. "Leave her with me. I'll have her done by Tuesday next."

"That's too late! We have to go back to America tomorrow!"

"I'm sorry then." The woman handed Felicity-Emma back. "I can't get to it any sooner. I'm very busy, as you see."

Two other customers had come in. She went to attend to them.

"Don't worry, Jen," said Mom. "There are places like this in New York. We can have it done there. Let's go." Daddy was waiting for them outside.

"No, Mom, please, wait a second!" Jenny rushed after the doll-hospital woman, through the store and through a door in the back clearly marked "No Admittance."

She found herself in a small workroom. In the middle was a table with arms and legs spread out, and dolls' heads without bodies, and dolls' bodies without heads. There were also scissors, pots of glue, spools of twine, pairs of pliers, sharp hooks, and other tools. And there were round things that looked like knee joints. And small things—ears! And glass things that at first Jenny thought were marbles—but no, they were eyeballs.

Jenny shuddered and tightened her hold on Felicity-Emma.

The owner was taking a doll that had been repaired off a shelf to return to a customer. She stood with her back to Jenny; she did not know that anyone was there.

"Ahem," said Jenny.

The owner wheeled around. "Can't you read? Didn't you see the sign?"

"I'm sorry. I just had to ask you again, couldn't you *please* take the thing out of my doll's throat today? It's terribly important."

"It is? How so?" asked the owner mockingly, daring her to tell.

"It's a precious thing."

"Such as what?"

"If I tell you, will you take it out? Today?"

"You've made me curious. All right, I will. But since it's so precious, and you're in such a hurry for it, I'll have to ask twice my usual fee."

"How much will it cost?"

"Two pounds."

I still have one pound and thirty pence left, Jenny thought. Mom or Daddy will lend me the rest. She said, "All right." And she told, in a hushed voice, what it was she thought the doll had in her throat.

"You don't say!" The woman took the doll from her and plonked her down on the shelf.

Felicity-Emma, be all right! Jenny wished with every hope she had in her.

Back in the store, where Mom waited impatiently, the owner wrote out the receipt and said, "Be here at five. I close at five thirty."

"Seven hours and five minutes to go," Jenny figured, walking along between her parents, "four hundred and twenty-five minutes. That's,"—she did the arithmetic in her head—"twenty-five thousand two hundred, no, twenty-five thousand five hundred seconds till I see her again."

She and her parents went through the Natural History Museum, which was huge, and through the Victoria and Albert Museum, which was enormous. Then they had lunch. Then they went into Kensington Gardens where, to Jenny's dismay, there was still another, the London Museum, into which they also went. She did not complain. This was their last day in London, and she owed it to her parents not to spoil it for them. But silently she counted the seconds going by. And whatever fossil, animal skeleton, tapestry, or historical document her real eyes were looking at, her mind's eye was riveted to dolls' eyes, ears, heads, arms, legs, and bodies scattered on the doll-hospital table.

Finally, finally, at a quarter to five, they were on a bus headed back to the Brompton Road.

The bus stopped a short distance from the doll hospital, but it seemed longer to Jenny than the total lengths of museum floors, pavement, and park paths she had walked today. And the nearer she got, the more clearly she pictured worst having come to worst: Felicity-Emma in pieces, unputtable together. The owner, gruffly saying she was sorry, she had done her best . . .

They were there, they went in.

Felicity-Emma sat on a shelf. She looked fine. Jenny ran and took her down.

"The operation was successful," said the owner. "Two pounds, if you please."

"Isn't that rather expensive?" said Daddy, paying seventy pence of it. Jenny paid the rest.

"It's very reasonable, under the circumstances," said the owner.

"What circumstances?" Daddy asked.

In answer, the owner took a little ball of crinkled-up tissue paper out of her pocket.

Jenny's hand trembled as she took it from her.

She uncrinkled the paper. And there it was—the size of a dewdrop, clear as a pool with the sun shining on it, of an extraordinary greenness, astonishingly bright.

Her parents bent close to see.

"It looks like an emerald," said Mom. "It's perfectly beautiful! Did you know all along it was in the doll?"

"Who put it there? To whom does it belong?" asked Daddy.

"I'll keep it in my pocketbook for now, if you want me to."

"No, Mom, I want to hold it. I'll tell you about it later."

They went back to the hotel to wash and change

for dinner. Jenny decided to wear her most festive dress. It was dark blue—not navy, more like the color of the night sky. It had billowy sleeves and a wide, graceful skirt with pockets in it.

When she had it on, Mom came in. In her hand was the silver box with the rose on it from Bermondsey. She said, "I thought you might want to borrow this to keep the emerald in."

"Yes, that's just perfect. Thanks, Mom." Jenny put the emerald in and slipped the box into the left-hand pocket of her dress.

"Are you sure you want to carry it around with you, Jen? Daddy thought maybe we should leave it in the hotel safe while we're out."

"We don't have to do that! It's so tiny, who'd want to steal it?" Jenny put her hand in her pocket, closing it tight over the box. "It'll be fine in here."

Nineteen

For their last dinner in London, Jenny's father had made reservations at an elegant restaurant right on the river Thames. They sat near a window and could see barges and sightseeing boats go by.

There were flowers and a candle on their table, heavy silverware, big cloth napkins, service plates, just for decoration until plates with food arrived, and three different glasses at every place setting for water and white and red wine. And every time the waiter approached, he bowed to them.

In these festive surroundings, while her parents had cocktails and Jenny had one without the whisky in it, Jenny explained to them about the emerald.

She began by telling that in Daddy's family a ring with the emerald in it had been handed down from his great-grandmother to his grandmother, to his mother, to Aunt Trudl; but that when Aunt Trudl got it, she was only twelve, instead of eighteen, like the others all had been.

"Why was that?" Daddy asked.

"Because she was going away, and your parents wanted her to have it, and to feel more grown up. But wait, I haven't told you Mariedl's tale yet. Mariedl was your grandmother's housekeeper." And Jenny told them the strange tale.

"Phew, that's scary," said Mom.

"It was to Trudl," said Jenny, thinking, It was to me, too.

"Anyway, Trudl got the ring as a going-away present when she left Vienna. To make her feel as though she was older than she really was, and so she shouldn't be too homesick. But she was very homesick. She also missed her dolls a lot. She wished she had brought one. And she wished that Mark Sanderson would give her one he had that he didn't even want any more. But he wouldn't. Not even as a trade for the ring. Not even when she told him the emerald in it was magic. He just laughed at her. And he traded the doll to his sister for a goldfish. So then Trudl felt really awful. She made believe she believed all that stuff about the emerald. And pretty soon she did believe it. So then she beswore—is that a word?"

"I don't think so," Daddy said. "But go on."

"Well, she begged the emerald really hard, she practically prayed to it to make the goldfish die. And the next day the goldfish was really dead. So then she really believed all that about the devil and the magic even more, especially the evil magic. And she felt terrible, and scared of what other, still more evil, things the emerald might make happen—"

The waiter came. Jenny had to stop while he took their orders.

"Now comes the secret part," she continued when the waiter had bowed himself away. "I shouldn't tell it." For the first time since getting Felicity-Emma back, her hand went up, a fingernail into her mouth. "I shouldn't even know it myself."

"You can't leave us on tenterhooks like that, Jenny," said Mom.

Daddy put his hand on Mom's arm. "It's up to Jenny. She doesn't have to tell us anything she doesn't want to."

Jenny felt torn between wanting to tell and not wanting to.

"Just tell me this," said Mom. "Is the secret part how the emerald got inside the doll?"

"Yes. I don't even know myself how it did. I only guessed."

"Well, I've been doing some guessing of my own," said Daddy. "Here's what *I* guessed: Once Trudl talked herself into believing all those things about the emerald, she couldn't trust herself with it any more. Somehow she managed to pry it out of its setting—that must have been hard to do. Then she put it in the doll's mouth, which is open just about wide enough."

"That's what I guessed, too," said Jenny.

"You did better than guess, you got it back,"

said Daddy. "So, Jenny, here's to you. For doing something rare and difficult." He clinked glasses with her.

"What do you mean?" asked Jenny.

"I mean rediscovering an important part of Aunt Trudl's past."

A twinge of the familiar guilt assailed her. She thought, I didn't rediscover it, Murrna did. . . . But her father didn't mean the copybook, he didn't even know about that. He meant all that she had found by going to Twiford. He's right about that, she started to think.

Daddy patted her hand. Mom beamed. They felt proud of her. Jenny started to feel proud of herself.

Then she asked, "But what do you really think about that stuff about the devil and the magic and all that?"

"You know what we think," said Mom.

Daddy laughed. "As my mother used to say, it's L—"

"*Larifari*," said Jenny.

"I didn't know you knew that word," Daddy said.

"What does it mean?" asked Mom.

Nonsense, Jenny wanted to answer in a casual voice. But instead, out of her mouth came the other word, "*Blödsinn*." The way she said it, it sounded a lot like "blood" and "sin." She felt herself turning red, blood rushing to her face, felt not proud of herself now, but scared, she wasn't sure exactly why or of what.

"Both those words mean nonsense," Daddy explained to Mom. Then he lifted his glass again. "I hereby propose another toast," he said loudly, boisterously. "To disbelief in *Blödsinn*—"

CRASH!

The busboy, clearing away the service plates, had jostled Daddy's arm just then. Daddy had let the glass fall. It shattered to pieces on the floor. The remains of the cocktail had spilled on his shirt. A reddish-brown stain spread across his chest.

The busboy excused himself in a frightened voice and dabbed at the stain with a napkin. Then he ducked under the table, to pick up the pieces of glass, but really more to hide from the waiter who approached with wrathful steps.

The waiter apologized in pompous tone on behalf of the entire establishment while hauling the busboy out from under the table and holding onto him by the back of the collar.

"Let him go," said Jenny's father, "don't give him a hard time, please, it wasn't his fault. Just bring us our dinner, all right?"

"As you wish, sir." The waiter released the busboy, and with redoubled bowing went to bring the food.

This restaurant was famous for its saddle of lamb with jellied mint sauce. They had ordered that.

When it arrived, Jenny wasn't hungry for it any-more. The lamb was pink—bloody, she thought. The mint sauce was so bright green and gleaming, it was like a mockery of the emerald's color.

The silver box in her pocket was pressing down on her thigh. The skin there felt suddenly irri-tated, almost painful. She shifted around in her chair. Awful thoughts came into her head: Daddy shouldn't have made that toast. Then that cocktail wouldn't have spilled . . . Her eyes kept getting drawn to the stain on his shirt. He might just as well have dared it, "Emerald, do your worst!" And who knows what much, much worse things than making somebody spill a drink it can do? Oh, I was wrong, I should have let it stay where Trudl hid it, where it couldn't do any harm. . . . What if its evil is making harm come to Felicity-Emma—right this minute while I'm sitting here forcing down lamb with mint so my parents won't ask me what's wrong?

Through the rest of the meal and on the way back to the hotel, she felt afraid for Felicity-Emma. She almost already saw her not in the least all right anymore . . . but with cracks and dents in her porcelain cheeks and forehead, with a bro-ken eyelid, chipped teeth, her hair coming loose, and her head lolling on her shoulders . . . with the life gone out of her, now that the emerald was out, now that it could do harm again.

When they got back, Mr. Fitzsimmons greeted them heartily, especially Jenny. He asked if they had enjoyed their last evening out in London. Daddy started telling him where they had been.

"Can I please have my key?" Jenny interrupted.

She was so in the throes of her fears, she did not notice the hurt look on Mr. Fitzsimmons's face that she did not say good-bye. She merely grabbed her key from him and rushed up the stairs two at a time to see about Felicity-Emma.

Twenty

She snapped the light on in her room and
swooped up Felicity-Emma from the bed.
Felicity-Emma opened her eyes. She was fine, exactly as Jenny had left her.

I was crazy to worry like that, Jenny thought.
She took the box out of her pocket and opened it.
The emerald looked harmless and beautiful, glis-
tening in the lamplight.

She went to bed and turned the light off. Bong,
bong, bong, bong, the church bell nearby tolled a
quarter past eleven.

She thought, In twelve hours we'll be at Heath-
row Airport. In thirteen and a quarter hours we'll
be on the plane. And then, New York . . . Aunt
Trudl hadn't said she was meeting them at the airport. They'd have to get home to West End Avenue in the limousine or somehow. But then, but
then . . . Jenny tried to picture the look on Aunt
Trudl's face when she saw what Jenny was bringing back.

To Jenny's dismay, Aunt Trudl's face would not

come right. All kinds of other pictures in her mind kept interfering: Trudl as she'd looked in the photograph, wearing her poppy dress, smiling for the camera . . . The face of a clock with the hands turning backward, as the clock hands really would tomorrow, going back to America, when time would turn back . . . And herself, ten days ago, flopped on Aunt Trudl's bed, reading the copybook. The guilt pangs about that were back.

She tried to change the scene, to concentrate on Aunt Trudl's cheery living room with the sun pouring in on all the plants, and the twenty-three throw cushions on the couch. "I used to try to stack those up into a tower to the ceiling when I was little," she said under her breath to Felicity-Emma, talking to her the way she used to, to April and Esther, when she was much younger. "And wait till you see the cats—Murrna, Mephisto, and my cat, Apricot Jones, and Augusta, my tur—" No use, she felt silly, talking like that. And when she mentioned Augusta, a worse picture came into her mind: of the turtle, dead as a stone.

This picture would not fade.

She sat up in bed, turned the light on, asked herself, How can I bring the emerald back there when I can't be sure it might not do some harm like that? How can I make sure—? She thought of Daddy's toast again, and the stain spreading over his shirt. She felt unnerved. I have to figure out what to do.

Instantly an idea came to her, complete with

rhymed incantation. It was so horrible, she could almost not believe she had thought it up on her own. . . . No, no, the emerald must have sent it into her head! In her mind's eye she saw Nelson, a feathery lump motionless on the floor of his cage—dead proof of the emerald's evil! And the incantation went like this:

> *Emerald, with your magic might,*
> *Kill the canary by midnight!*

Jenny felt nauseous. She thought, If that happens, I'll throw the emerald away. . . . But that wouldn't bring Nelson back to life, or make Mr. Fitzsimmons feel any better. I'd hate myself. Even if I became a veterinarian and specialized in canaries and saved hundreds of canaries' lives, I still would not forgive myself.

What if just having thought Nelson dead was proof of the emerald's magic? What if the thought was already starting to turn real, and Nelson falling from his perch that moment—"Oh, no!"

She ran into the bathroom. She only retched, she didn't vomit. She felt wobbly. She sat down on the edge of the bathtub. What am I doing to myself? I have to get hold of myself, stop thinking crazy things . . . It's *not* going to happen. But she could not be sure. Not until midnight had come and gone.

She took deep breaths, drank a sip of water.

The church bell tolled eleven thirty. A whole half hour to wait!

She went back into the room. She took out her sketch pad and yellow pastel. She sat down at the desk and tried to draw. At least it would make the time pass. And she'd have something to remember Nelson by—not that, if worst came to worst, she'd ever be able to forget him ever for a moment. . . .

She tried to draw a bird outline. Her hand shook. The line came out wavy.

She tried again. The line was even wavier. She thought, If the emerald's magic helped me last night when I was making a picture of the emerald, it definitely isn't helping me now. I have to get hold of myself, she told herself again, clutching the pastel hard between thumb and index finger, bearing down hard on the paper. There, that was better, now at least the line was firm—No! The line came to a sudden stop as the pastel broke in two.

Jenny felt numb with fright. She let her head drop with a thud onto the desk, onto the pad. She shut her eyes and tried to shut everything else out of her mind. And she implored the emerald, desparately, fervently, Let no harm come to Nelson! But who knew if it was not already too late for that now?

At the stroke of a quarter to twelve, she put the night-blue dress back on. Before, she had been proud of how festive it looked. She didn't care about that now. Now, the only reason she wore it was, it was the closest thing to black.

She put her socks and shoes back on. She brushed her hair smooth. And she waited some more.

At last the bell started tolling midnight. The silences in between tolls seemed eternal. Every toll coincided with a pang in her chest. Finally, finally, twelve!

Outwardly, thank goodness, she was under control. She took her key. It wouldn't do to forget it this time.

Inwardly she wished, If only I believed in God, then I could have been praying all this time, I could be praying now, going down these stairs . . .

Going down the last flight, she implored the nighttime stillness, "Please, please let me hear singing!"

But she heard no sound, only the clunk of the elevator reaching the ground, the squeak of its iron door opening.

The lobby was dark, except for the lamp on Mr. Fitzsimmons's desk. By the dim light it gave, Jenny saw Mr. Fitzsimmons sitting there, his bald head slumped down—grieving? Weeping? The birdcage stood before him, covered with a dark cloth.

And Jenny thought, It happened. Worst came to worst, just as I thought.

Mr. Fitzsimmons raised his head, saw her, stood up, came toward her. "Why, Miss Hurnthile!

You're as white in the face as if you'd seen a ghost! Is something the matter?"

"Is Nelson okay?"

He looked at her wonderingly for a second. Then he whisked the dark cover off the cage.

Nelson lifted his head out from under his wing.

"There's a good fellow, wake up, that's right. Miss Hurnthile's come down to say good-bye to us, didn't I tell you she would? 'E was just 'aving forty winks, Miss Hurnthile. Yes, 'e's okay, 'e's in the pink." Mr. Fitzsimmons laughed, and corrected himself, "Well, 'ardly pink, but feeling fine. Why shouldn't 'e be?"

"No reason!" Jenny laughed too. She had never felt so relieved and thankful for anything in her whole life.

"Why don't you give Miss Hurnthile a song?" Mr. Fitzsimmons coaxed Nelson.

Nelson gave a chirp.

"Not like that! Sing to 'er properly!"

Nelson wouldn't and wouldn't. After much coaxing, he consented to give a succession of short chirps, seven in a row.

Jenny set them to words in her head: "All things bright and beautiful—"

"That's not enough for a farewell performance," Mr. Fitzsimmons reproached the canary.

"That's okay," Jenny said. She thanked Mr. Fitzsimmons for having been so nice to her during her stay. "Thank you, too, Nelson," she said, and she didn't just mean for the start of the song.

171

Then she and Mr. Fitzsimmons said good-bye and shook hands, and he wished her a good trip home.

In the elevator, going up, she felt kind of giddy, like in the plane, as though she were rising up on her own, from feeling as light as air now that the great load of fear was off her. And as she rose, the start of that hymn, to which she didn't know the tune, got changed around a little and put together with some other words in her head and became a new song to a tune she made up herself:

> *Two things bright and beautiful,*
> *One green, one lemony,*
> *Are fine, are perfectly okay,*
> *And that's just great with me!*

Back in her room, she felt sort of like writing the song down, but then thought, No, it would look dumb on paper. It wasn't those jumbled-together words or that tune she wanted to hold onto. It was the mood of it, how great she'd felt down there with Nelson and Mr. Fitzsimmons, and in the elevator, and how great she felt right this minute, much too good to just go to bed and straight to sleep.

She did go to bed, but with her box of pastels. She propped her sketch pad on her knees and, wondering what in the world would come out, set this mood to shapes and colors.

She started with yellow, of course. The two

halves of the broken pastel were both perfectly good. She used the bigger one first. She held it loosely instead of pressing so hard. With fingers and wrist relaxed, she let the pastel have its way— well, almost. She did guide it some. And it made a kind of bird outline, not exact, not even neat, but suggesting a bird well enough, with its beak pointing up and wide open, as though it were pouring out a song.

She colored the bird canary, of course, blending white in with yellow to make it lemony.

She let pink streamers, curlicues, star shapes, and round shapes with tails, like musical notes, pour out of its beak in all directions. Then she put whatever other shapes all around that seemed to go together and whatever color looked happy, light, and bright. Lastly, in all four corners, she put roundnesses of green, sending out radiances all over the place.

There, it was done. She didn't give a thought to what anyone—even Mom—would say about it. She, Jenny, liked it, she thought it was good.

Exhausted now, but feeling terrific, she put the pad and pastels in her suitcase. She lay down, and the instant after she turned the light off, she was fast asleep.

Twenty-One

It was six o'clock Sunday evening. The New York sky for once looked sparklingly clear, without smoke or smog. Jenny stood at her window at home, with Felicity-Emma, looking out at the Hudson River, a rare shade of dark blue tonight, topped with a froth of white caps.

The sun still stood high over New Jersey on the other side. In London, though, it would be midnight now. Jenny was tired. She put Felicity-Emma to bed in a chair with Esther and April, and went to bed herself.

The door opened a crack. Aunt Trudl peeked in.

"Aunt Trudl, come in, I'm not asleep yet!"

"Good." She came over to the bed. She held something in her hands. "I wanted to give you this."

"The copybook! When did you find it?"

"Yesterday. I needed a book from up there, and sneezed from all the dust, so I started to dust the shelf—and there it was. I hadn't seen it in so long!

First I was surprised it had so little dust on it, compared to the other books. Then I remembered—you were so upset the day you left, and hinted around, and tried to tell me, you'd found it and read it—oh Jenny!"

Jenny could read Aunt Trudl's blue-gray-green-eyed smile more clearly than any words on any page. It said, I know what you've been through. It said, We two are even closer now than we were before.

She put the copybook in Jenny's hands. "You may want to use the empty pages in it." She kissed Jenny on both cheeks. "Good night, see you tomorrow." And she went out the door.

Jenny could not think of sleeping now. She turned to the page where she had left off, where Trudl did that most "seecret" thing, and said that rhyme to the emerald, ending with "But still be mine."

Below that, the page was bare and bumpy as though it had gotten wet.

She cried on it, Jenny thought. Maybe she was already sorry. She probably already had a hunch she would have to leave the doll behind. So she thought she'd never see the emerald again. . . .

Jenny got a pen out of her desk drawer. She drew a line underneath the rhyme, put the day's date, and wrote underneath that, feeling proud and happy, "Now the emerald *is* hers again."

She turned the page and read on:

NEW WORDS:

(Mr. Sanderson asked me, how are my new words coming along, so I shall write some down again.)

1. GYMKHANA. *That is a very hard word. It means, riding contest. Pam was in one, riding Midnight. She won three prizes. Afterward she was more jolly pleased with herself than ever.*

2. BLOOMING. *That sometimes has nothing to do with what flowers do, but means the same as bloody, only not quite so rude.*

3. BLIGHTER. *Someone awful. For example, Mr. Chamberlain. He is the Prime Minister of England. "That blighter," Mr. Sanderson sayd about him. Then Mrs. Sanderson sayd, "Hush, dear, not in front of the children."*

4. WIRELESS. *That means radio.*

September 7

I heard on the wireless that Hitler wants the Sudetenland. That belongs to Czechoslovakia. It made me think of a song Upstairs-Lieselotte taught me. Her parents were already Nazis before Hitler took over Austria, so she already knew all the Nazi songs before. That one goes, "We will go marching farther, Till everything smashes to bits, And today belongs to us Germany, and tomorrow the whole, whole world." I am afraid that it is coming true.

September 30

Mr. "Blighter" Chamberlain came today back from Munich, it sayd on the wireless and in the newspaper. He went there to visit Hitler. And now he is letting Hitler have Czechoslovakia. Mr. Sanderson shouted, "The bloody swine," right in front of Mark and me. Then he sayd I shoud not listen so much to the wireless. And he sent us out.

October 15

I have settled in nicely at school, sayd Miss Huddleston. She is head mistress. She has a small fat black-and-white dog called Reggie. He is allowed to be in the classrooms and everywhere. My form is the Upper B's. Mark is in the Lower B's. Pam would be in the Lower A's. But she has gone to boarding school. And she took Felicity-Emma—after all her talk that she is too old for dolls! And after her promiss to me! I do miss Felicity-Emma. Luckily Nirob is sitting on the desk where he can watch me write.

At school I like History the best. We study Magna Carta and about King John. I get on rather well with Mark these days. He wishes he was older and could be in the R.A.F. That is the Royal Air Force. Many people talk

about, will there be a war? I hope there will.
But not while my parents are in Vienna still.

And that was all. The remaining pages were blank—or seemed to be. It doesn't have an ending, thought Jenny drowsily.

The next thing she knew, she was back at the airport, holding something she wanted Aunt Trudl to take. Aunt Trudl, in her horseblankety bathrobe, had her back to Jenny and would not turn around. "I told you not to bring me any presents," she said.

"I didn't," said Jenny. "This is different, you'll see!"

Finally Aunt Trudl took it. And when she opened it, it was the garden from the sidewalk, only now it was real, with the lawn and all the summer flowers. Ballou and Rufus chased around playing tag; and it made perfect sense that one was from then and one from now. Grown-up Pam and Aunt Trudl walked around arm in arm. Why aren't I in the garden, though? Jenny wondered, feeling left out of her own dream. Just then a boy jumped out at her from behind a tree, so she was in it after all. He stopped and picked her a nasturtium leaf. "You can eat it," he said. "It's better than noodle strudel!" And in the dream this was both kind and funny, and everybody laughed.

Twenty-Two

Next morning, Monday, not a church bell nearby but the doorbell woke Jenny, and she realized she was home and who was there. She grabbed something out of her suitcase and ran to the door.

"Hi, Jenny, I know I'm early, but I couldn't wait any more! Did you have a great time?"

"Hi, Nancy. I'm glad you came early, yes I did. Here. This is for you, do you like it?"

Nancy Saradian loved the blue velvet drawstring bag from Bermondsey. She stayed while Jenny dressed and had breakfast. Then they walked to school together, and back together at three.

Then Jenny went up to Aunt Trudl's.

She picked up all three cats in turn and stroked and petted them hello. She gave Apricot Jones the plush ball with the squeak in it.

A sunbeam streamed in through the window, ending in a pool of sunlight on the floor in which Augusta bathed. Jenny sat down and shared the sunlight with her and touched her on the face.

Then she went into the kitchen. Aunt Trudl's

hands were covered with eggy flour and bread-
crumb mixture; she was breading veal cutlets—
Wiener_ Schnitzel—for tonight's dinner. Jenny
peeled and sliced cucumbers very thin for salad.
They talked as they worked, and continued talking long after the preparations for dinner were
done.

Then Aunt Trudl went to take a bath.

Jenny had some things she wanted to write into
the copybook. She had brought it along.

"Use my desk if you want to," Aunt Trudl
called.

Jenny wrote: -

> *It poured when we left London, but I like
> leaving places in the rain.*
>
> *In the airplane, higher than the clouds, I
> felt terrific again. But then I got impatient
> for it to be over. I still couldn't imagine how
> Aunt Trudl would look when she saw
> Felicity-Emma. And that bothered me.*
>
> *When we finally got over Kennedy Air-
> port, our plane had to circle around and
> around. A bunch of other planes were sup-
> posed to land ahead of us, the pilot said.*
>
> *When we finally landed, we had to wait
> ages for our suitcases, then for the customs
> inspector to open them up and inspect them.*
>
> *Mom had the silver box with the emerald
> in her pocketbook. She showed it to the cus-
> toms man and started explaining how old it*

was and all. He said that was okay, we didn't need to pay duty on it.

Finally we were through customs. Daddy said, "Now we have to see about a bus or limousine."

"There's Aunt Trudl!" I saw her! I ran. She was way at the other end of the airport building.

I was carrying Felicity-Emma. When I got closer, I held her up and yelled, "Aunt Trudl, look!"

Now she saw me. She ran too. The place was really crowded. We bumped into a lot of people. I stepped on someone's foot. Somebody's pocketbook banged into me, but I didn't even feel it.

The first thing we did when we got to each other was, we hugged each other. Next thing, she recognized Felicity-Emma. Right away. I didn't have to say anything.

One reason I am writing this down is, I wanted to tell what she looked like when she realized it was her. But now I don't know how.

Some day I might try it in a picture. I wouldn't make it like a photograph of exactly how she looked then. I can't draw that well. But even if I could, I wouldn't do it that way. I'd do it sort of like the picture I made the last night in London, but with different shapes and colors, of course. They wouldn't look like anything much in themselves. But if the picture turned out good, together they could make you see the whole bunch of feelings Aunt Trudl must have had at that moment. I know what they were, but I can't put them into words.

Anyway, I said, "That's right, it's Felicity-Emma, it really is!" I also said, I didn't care how stupid it sounded, "She's still alive!"

Aunt Trudl touched her on the cheeks. She said, "Yes, I can see that." Then we both laughed because of how serious we were being.

Then I said, "Wait till you see what I brought you!"

"A present? Didn't I tell you not to?" She wagged her finger and pretended to be mad.

"It isn't a present. And you'll like it, you'll see."

Then my parents came. They were really glad to see her too, and said how great of her to surprise us like that.

Then we went to a parking lot pretty far away where she had parked Silverman's station wagon that he had lent her. On the way there I asked Mom to give me the she-knew-what, and she did.

Aunt Trudl wanted Mom or Daddy to drive if they weren't too tired, because she doesn't like driving in lots of traffic.

Mom drove. Daddy sat in front with her.

Aunt Trudl sat in back with me. And I gave her the silver box. I told her the box was a present from Mom and Daddy.

"It's beautiful! I love it, especially the rose." She leaned forward and put kisses from her fingers onto the backs of their heads. "Thank you both, a lot."

Then she opened it. I won't even try to describe the look on her face. She kind of gasped and smiled at the same time. And she asked me, "How did you get it out?"

"I couldn't. We had to take her to a doll hospital. The woman there took it out."

There was a whirr in my head from being up in the air so long, and I felt funny being back on the ground, and that it wasn't night here yet even though I'd been awake so many hours. I didn't want to tell the whole story then. It would have come out very jumbled up.

Aunt Trudl knows me pretty well. She pulled my head down on her shoulder. "Close your eyes now. We'll have lots of time to talk, later."

That's what we were doing, in the kitchen, just now.

Jenny had come to the bottom of a left-hand page. After that there were four more pages.

She was done writing, but didn't want to get up from here. It was so pleasant sitting at this big desk in this quiet room. She started doodling. She doodled a little bird into the right-hand corner of the page she had just finished writing. Then she doodled a small semicircle at the top of the facing page. She gave it feet with tiny scales and claws. She was just about to give it a head and tail and make it be a turtle when she noticed writing from the next page showing through.

Hey, I thought there wasn't anything more in here, she thought, and turned—and found the next page and two remaining ones covered with Trudl's small script. Wow, I must have really had jet lag last night, that I didn't even notice those pages were stuck together, she thought. And she read:

November 21, 1938

I have not felt like writing in here for a long time. But now I have my letter that I yearned for, and I want that to be the last thing in this copybook. I allready read it twenty times and know it by heart. I translated parts of it to Mrs. Sanderson and Mark. Mark said he'd be thrilled to bits if he could go somewhere in a boat.

Mrs. Sanderson said, "I'm so glad for you, Trudl, dear. I shall miss you dreadfully. So will Mark." Mark made one of his faces. But later he said, yes, he woud.

Mrs. Sanderson said Pam woud be sorry that it's the middle of term and she can't

come home to say good-bye. But I think she'll
be jolly glad, or she'd have to say something
about that promiss. I do mind about Felicity-
Emma, and will never forget her. But now
that my letter has come, nothing, nothing can
make me anymore feel bad.

Now, because I promised Mr. Sanderson
not to write anything in this copybook in German, I shall translate my letter into English:

"Dear Trudl, heart's bundle (that sounds
dotty in English, but in German it's a pet
name people often say):

I have wonderful news for us all, my dar-
ling: Our waiting time is soon over. Our
quota numbers have come up. Your father
was today at the American consulate. Now
we have our visas! If you don't know what
consulates or visas or quota numbers are, that
makes nothing, break not your head about
such things. Important only is: Soon we will
not anymore be separated. Soon we will be a
family again, and a bigger one, as you will
see.

"On December first, we will sail for America. We will be on the H.M.S. Aquitania.
(H.M.S. means His Majesty's Ship. I thought
at first it was King George the Sixth's own
ship when he goes somewhere, but Mark said,
no, all British ships are called H.M.S.) They
say it is as big as three whole city streets.
That is so big that nobody on it gets seasick.

185

Doris Orgel ·

"Vati and I will arrive in London, at Victoria Station, on November 27th at noon if the train is punctual. I am sure the Sandersons, who have already been so kind to you, will bring you to meet us at the train, or if not, then to the hotel where we will stay. It is the Swiss Cottage Hotel. They will know where that is. We will stay there till the twenty-ninth. Then we go by train to Southampton. That is on the sea, and there the boat will be.

"Give please our best regards to Mr. and Mrs. Sanderson and also to the children. Tell them how much we feel gratitude to them. We count the hours till we see you, heart's child. (That sounds dotty too, but in German not.) We embrace and kiss you thousand times.

"Your always loving Mutti.
"P.S. I will have a surprise for you."

Jenny finished reading. But she stayed sitting there, elbows on the desk, chin propped in her hands.

Then the bell rang, startling her.

She went and opened the door. "Hi, Jen," said her father.

"Daddy! It was you!"

"What's so extraordinary about that? Were you expecting the man in the moon?"

"I don't mean now!"

"What do you mean?" he asked, bewildered.

Jenny took him into the bedroom-study and showed him the translation of his mother's letter in the copybook.

He took a long time reading it.

Then Mom came. Then Silverman came. Mom gave him the walrus. He liked it so much, he put it in the center of the table. Then they all had dinner.

In the next six weeks, three things happened that Jenny thought belonged in the copybook. She wrote them down on the only blank page left, the one at the top of which she had started to doodle the turtle:

The emerald is in a new gold ring now. Silverman had it made for Aunt Trudl. She wears it all the time.

Today I got a package from Mrs. Harwood with clothes in it for Felicity: a white blouse with a sailor collar. A straw hat with pink ribbons. A green pleated skirt. A lavender taffeta party dress that rustles. Three pairs of ruffled underpants. And real riding breeches.

Today Mom and I went over to Madison Avenue, to Tarcheff's Frame Store, to pick up something she'd ordered. I wondered what it could be. She usually frames her paintings herself, plain, with just four pieces of wood around them. I was really surprised when I saw what it was: my picture of the emerald, that I made that night before I went to Twiford. I thought I'd left it in the desk drawer in the hotel. But Mom packed it. It looks really good in its gold-colored frame with glass over it, ~~almost~~ as if a real artist had made it.

Mom hung it up in her studio. She says she likes to look at it while she works.

BESTSELLERS FROM
LAUREL-LEAF LIBRARY

☐ **ARE YOU THERE, GOD? IT'S ME, MARGARET**
by Judy Blume $1.25 0419-39

☐ **THE BOY WHO COULD MAKE HIMSELF
DISAPPEAR** by Kin Platt $1.25 0837-25

☐ **THE CHOCOLATE WAR**
by Robert Cormier $1.25 4459-08

☐ **DEENIE** by Judy Blume $1.25 3259-02

☐ **DURANGO STREET**
by Frank Bonham $1.25 2183-13

☐ **FAIR DAY, AND ANOTHER STEP BEGUN**
by Katie Letcher Lyle $1.25 5968-09

☐ **IF I LOVE YOU, AM I TRAPPED FOREVER?**
by M. E. Kerr $1.25 4320-05

☐ **I'LL GET THERE, IT BETTER BE
WORTH THE TRIP** by John Donovan ... $1.25 3980-08

☐ **I'M REALLY DRAGGED BUT NOTHING
GETS ME DOWN** by Nat Hentoff .... 95¢ 3988-26

☐ **I WILL GO BAREFOOT ALL SUMMER FOR YOU**
by Katie Letcher Lyle $1.25 4327-08

☐ **JANE EMILY** by Patricia Clapp .... 75¢ 4185-09

☐ **THE OUTSIDERS** by S. E. Hinton $1.25 6769-40

☐ **THE PIGMAN** by Paul Zindel $1.25 6970-11

☐ **THAT WAS THEN, THIS IS NOW**
by S. E. Hinton $1.25 8652-12

At your local bookstore or use this handy coupon for ordering:

Dell | **DELL BOOKS**
P.O. BOX 1000, PINEBROOK, N.J. 07058

Please send me the books I have checked above. I am enclosing $_____
(please add 35¢ per copy to cover postage and handling). Send check or money
order—no cash or C.O.D.'s. Please allow up to 8 weeks for shipment.

Mr/Mrs/Miss_____

Address_____

City_____ State/Zip_____

Outstanding Laurel-Leaf Fiction for Young Adult Readers

☐ **A LITTLE DEMONSTRATION OF AFFECTION**
  Elizabeth Winthrop $1.25
A 15-year-old girl and her older brother find themselves turning to each other to share their deepest emotions.

☐ **M.C. HIGGINS THE GREAT**
  Virginia Hamilton $1.25
Winner of the Newbery Medal, the National Book Award and the Boston Globe-Horn Book Award, this novel follows M.C. Higgins' growing awareness that both choice and action lie within his power.

☐ **PORTRAIT OF JENNIE**
  Robert Nathan $1.25
Robert Nathan interweaves touching and profound portraits of all his characters with one of the most beautiful love stories ever told.

☐ **THE MEAT IN THE SANDWICH**
  Alice Bach $1.25
Mike Lefcourt dreams of being a star athlete, but when hockey season ends, Mike learns that victory and defeat become hopelessly mixed up.

☐ **Z FOR ZACHARIAH**
  Robert C. O'Brien $1.25
This winner of an Edgar Award from the Mystery Writers of America portrays a young girl who was the only human being left alive after nuclear doomsday—or so she thought.

At your local bookstore or use this handy coupon for ordering:

Dell | **DELL BOOKS**
P.O. BOX 1000, PINEBROOK, N.J. 07058

Please send me the books I have checked above. I am enclosing $_____
(please add 35¢ per copy to cover postage and handling). Send check or money order—no cash or C.O.D.'s. Please allow up to 8 weeks for shipment.

Mr/Mrs/Miss_____

Address_____

City_____State/Zip_____

"Unique in its uncompromising portrait of human cruelty and conformity."
—*School Library Journal*

THE CHOCOLATE WAR

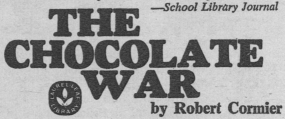

by Robert Cormier

A compelling combination of
Lord Of The Flies **and** ***A Separate Peace***

Jerry Renault, a New England high school student, is stunned by his mother's recent death and appalled by the way his father sleepwalks through life. At school, he resists the leader of a secret society by refusing to sell candies for the chocolate sale, wondering: Do I dare disturb the universe?

"Masterfully structured and rich in theme. . . . The action is well crafted, well timed, suspenseful; complex ideas develop and unfold with clarity."
—*The New York Times*

"Readers will respect the uncompromising ending."
—*Kirkus Reviews*

"Close enough to the reality of the tribal world of adolescence to make one squirm."—*Best Sellers*

Laurel-Leaf Fiction $1.25

At your local bookstore or use this handy coupon for ordering:

Dell **DELL BOOKS**   The Chocolate War $1.25 (94459-7)
P.O. BOX 1000, PINEBROOK, N.J. 07058

Please send me the above title. I am enclosing $_____
(please add 35¢ per copy to cover postage and handling). Send check or money order—no cash or C.O.D.'s. Please allow up to 8 weeks for shipment.

Mr/Mrs/Miss_____

Address_____

City_____State/Zip_____

*A Revealing Novel about Teenagers—
by a Teenager*

THE OUTSIDERS

by S. E. Hinton

"The Outsiders," a rough and swinging gang of teen-agers from the wrong side of the tracks, have little hope for the material pleasures of American life. Their mode of expression is violence—directed toward the group of privileged kids who are at once objects of their envy and their hatred. "Written by a most perceptive teenager. It attempts to communicate to adults their doubts, their dreams, and their needs."—*Book Week*

A Laurel-Leaf Paperback $1.25

At your local bookstore or use this handy coupon for ordering:

Dell	**DELL BOOKS**	The Outsiders $1.25 (96769-4)
	P.O. BOX 1000, PINEBROOK, N.J. 07058	

Please send me the above title. I am enclosing $_____
(please add 35¢ per copy to cover postage and handling). Send check or money order—no cash or C.O.D.'s. Please allow up to 8 weeks for shipment.

Mr/Mrs/Miss_____

Address_____

City_____ State/Zip_____